THE CHRISTIAN HERO

> To
> My Lord Tutour Dr Ellis
>
> With secret impulse thus do Streams return
> To that Capacious Ocean whence they're born:
> Oh Wou'd but Fortune come wth bounty fraught
> Proportion'd to ye mind wch thou hast taught!
> Till then let these unpolish'd leaves impart
> The Humble offering of a Gratefull Heart.
>
> Rich: Steele

FLYLEAF of the copy of the *Christian Hero* (second edition) presented by Steele to his tutor, Dr. Welbore Ellis. In the Dyce Library, Victoria and Albert Museum, South Kensington. See *Preface*, p. iii

THE CHRISTIAN HERO

By
RICHARD STEELE

*Edited with an
Introduction and a Bibliography
By* RAE BLANCHARD

OCTAGON BOOKS

A DIVISION OF FARRAR, STRAUS AND GIROUX

New York   1977

Originally published in 1932 by Oxford University Press

Reprinted 1977
by special arrangement with Oxford University Press

OCTAGON BOOKS
A DIVISION OF FARRAR, STRAUS & GIROUX, INC.
19 Union Square West
New York, N.Y. 10003

Library of Congress Cataloging in Publication Data

Steele, Richard, Sir, 1672-1729.
   The Christian hero.

   Reprint of the 1932 ed. published by Oxford University Press, London.
   Bibliography: p.
   1. Christian life.   I. Title.
PR3704.C5   1977   824'.5   77-22190
ISBN 0-374-97608-2

Printed in USA by
Thomson-Shore, Inc.
Dexter, Michigan

PREFACE

THIS volume is the result of study, conversation, and exchange of ideas which took place in the seminar rooms, the library, and the common room of Wieboldt Hall at the University of Chicago. The Introduction is an abridgement of one section of a dissertation presented in 1927 for the degree of Doctor of Philosophy. The work on the text and on the bibliography was also done at Chicago. I am glad of this opportunity to express publicly my appreciation of the pleasant and stimulating associations there which aroused my interest in Steele and the eighteenth century.

My grateful acknowledgements are due to the Librarians of the forty or more libraries who answered my inquiries concerning their copies of the *Christian Hero*; to the Henry E. Huntington Library for photostatic material; to the Library of the University of Chicago; and above all to the Library of the University of Texas, from which came, with almost incredible generosity, the loan of the sixteen editions of the *Christian Hero* in the Aitken Collection.

I wish to express my thanks to the Bibliographical Society for permission to reprint the bibliography, which first appeared in the *Transactions*, x (June 1929); and to the Victoria and Albert Museum, South Kensington, for permission to reproduce Steele's manuscript verses as frontispiece.

To Professor George Sherburn and Professor

Ronald S. Crane go my warmest thanks. Professor Sherburn, who first suggested that I undertake the edition, put his own fine collection of eighteenth-century books and pamphlets at my command. Professor Crane gave me constant and invaluable aid in every stage of the work even to the minutest particular. I am one of an increasing group of students who acknowledge gratefully his inspiring guidance.

R. B.

Goucher College
Baltimore, Maryland

CONTENTS

INTRODUCTION ix

A NOTE ON THE TEXT xxxi

THE CHRISTIAN HERO

    DEDICATION 3

    PREFACE 7

    CHAPTER I 13

    CHAPTER II 35

    CHAPTER III 49

    CHAPTER IV 69

BIBLIOGRAPHY 89

FACSIMILES

Fly-leaf of the copy of the *Christian Hero* presented by Steele to his tutor, Dr. Welbore Ellis . *Frontispiece*

Title-page of the Third Edition . . *Page* 1

INTRODUCTION

I

IN April, 1701,[1] was published the first reforming venture of the propagandist who was to become famous as Isaac Bickerstaff, the Spectator, and Nestor Ironside. It was the *Christian Hero: An Argument Proving that No Principles but Those of Religion are Sufficient to Make a Great Man* by Captain Richard Steele. He wrote it, he told his Colonel in the Dedication, while on duty as guard at the Tower. His fellow soldiers were the special readers for whom it was intended, and, as he explained many years later, the chief object of his reform was himself:

> He first became an Author when an Ensign of the Guards, a way of Life exposed to much Irregularity; and being thoroughly convinced of many things, of which he often repented, and which he more often repeated, he writ, for his own private Use, a little Book called the *Christian Hero*, with a design principally to fix upon his own Mind a strong Impression of Virtue and Religion, in opposition to a stronger Propensity toward unWarrantable Pleasures.[2]

The *Christian Hero* was, of course, related in a general way to the vast output, at the turn of the century, of reforming tracts on every possible subject. In particular, it was related to those tracts whose purpose was reform of the 'Universal and Destructive Torrent of Error and Pleasure' among the 'Men of Wit and Gallantry'.[3] But it was not in

[1] Advertised in the *Post Man* and the *Post Boy* for April 15–17.
[2] *Mr. Steele's Apology for Himself and His Writings* (1714), p. 80.
[3] Preface.

the vein of the numerous contemporary manuals of prayer and piety for young men, used so extensively as propaganda by the Society for the Reformation of Manners and by the religious societies. Such tracts as, for example, *The Young Man's Duty* by Richard Kidder (6th ed., 1695) and *War with the Devil or the Young Man's Conflict with the Powers of Darkness* by Benjamin Keach (10th ed., 1700) were quite different in design and purpose from Steele's reforming essay. Nor was it like the manuals by Anthony Horneck, written presumably for the religious societies of young men under his direction—*An Antidote Against a Careless Indifferency in Matters of Religion* (1694) and *The Happy Ascetic* (4th ed., 1699).

Steele's model had more dignity than these manuals of piety. It is to be found, rather, in the moral and psychological essay with religious colouring, which inquired into the principles of morality: into the nature of reason and the passions, the motives of conduct, and the relation of Christianity to right conduct. Typical examples of these essays, which also were designed for the reform of irreligion and which were particularly numerous in the latter years of the century, are *A Discourse upon the Nature and Faculties of Man* by Timothy Nourse (1686 and 1697); *L'art de se connoître soi-même* by Jacques Abbadie (1692), which had a popular English edition in the *Art of Knowing One-self or an Enquiry into the Sources of Morality* by Thomas Woodcock (1694 and 1698); and the *Government of the Passions* by Captain W. Ayloffe (1700), an adaptation of Senault's *De l'usage des passions*. The *Christian Hero*, while not identical in design with any one of these essays,

Introduction

shared their general purpose and their points of view. Steele's defence of Christianity over pagan morality was exactly that of Abbadie; and his views on the control of the passions were very similar to those of Ayloffe, who also addressed men of gallantry with the purpose of moralizing wit. Even the originality which might be claimed for the *Christian Hero* as a reforming tract written especially by a soldier for soldiers would probably be challenged, were the book extant, by William Morgan's *Religio Militis or a Souldier's Religion. Writ by a Field Officer in His Winter Quarters* (1695).[1]

From the very first, Steele's essay has been criticized for weaknesses in both subject-matter and style. The first critic, writing in 1702 in *A Comparison between the Two Stages*, was very severe:

'Tis a Chaos, 'tis a confusion of Thoughts, rude and indigested; . . . 'Tis Dated from the Tower-Guard, as a present to his Colonel, that his Colonel might think him even in time of Duty a very contemplative Soldier, and I suppose by the roughness of the Stile, he writ it there on the Butt-end of a Musquet.[2]

The reading public of the nineteenth century almost forgot it. At best it was remembered only as 'a valuable little manual';[3] it was apologized for as the writing of 'a theologian in liquor',[4] and it was even vaguely referred to by one historian as a poem.[5] In

[1] Listed in the *Term Catalogues* (ed. Arber), ii. 555 (June, 1695).
[2] pp. 161-3.
[3] Nathan Drake, *Essays, Biographical, Critical, and Historical, Illustrative of the Tatler, Spectator, and Guardian* (1805), i. 48.
[4] W. M. Thackeray, *English Humorists of the Eighteenth Century* (New York, 1900), pp. 113-14.
[5] Schlosser, *History of the Eighteenth Century* (1843), i. 102, as quoted by G. A. Aitken, *Life of Richard Steele* (1889), i. 66 n.

recent years it has suffered the fate of a minor essay overshadowed by its author's more famous works.

But in spite of the fact that it belongs to a genre of slight literary value and that it is marred in places by careless writing, the *Christian Hero* is worth reconsideration. There are fine passages in it which admirers of Steele regard as being among his best. It is interesting because it contains the initial expression of some of the ideas—for example, the defence of women and the denunciation of false honour and duelling—which he elaborated in his periodicals, and because his moral theory, his starting-point for two decades of corrective propaganda, is first outlined here. Moreover, the *Christian Hero* is historically important in that it contains a notable early discussion of benevolence, its origin and nature, a subject prominent in eighteenth-century thought. But the question of originality and intrinsic value apart, Steele's essay, which ran into twenty editions during the eighteenth century, cannot be ignored in the history of ideas. Steele himself thought well of it. In July, 1701, after its appearance in April, he published a second edition enlarged and carefully revised; and in 1710 he took the pains to revise it again for a third edition. From time to time, also, he incorporated portions of it in his periodicals.[1]

These are sufficient reasons for publishing a new edition of the *Christian Hero*—which has not been reprinted for more than a century—and for attempt-

---

[1] *Spectator*, Nos. 356 and 516; *Guardian*, Nos. 20 and 79; *Englishman* (first series), No. 48. See also the *Apology for Himself and His Writings*, pp. 46–7.

Introduction

ing an analysis of the ideas expressed in it and an interpretation of them by reference to the thought in Steele's background.

II

The general theme of the essay, as the title implies, is the superiority of religion over pagan philosophy as a moral guide for men of affairs. Steele was on the defensive. Aware of prejudices among his readers given to 'the Fashionable Vice of Exploding Religion',[1] he inquired tactfully into the reason why the 'Christian sneaks' in the imagination while the 'Heathen struts'. In spite of the 'Pompous Look Elegant Pens'[2] had given pagan heroes, he hoped to prove that the early Christians were the 'most truly Gallant and Heroick that ever appeared to Mankind'.[3] In the first chapter he discussed the lives of Cato, Caesar, and Brutus in order to demonstrate that their philosophy failed them in times of crisis. In the second, he told of the heroic elements in the life of Christ. The third eulogized the precepts and lives of the early Christians, especially of Saint Paul, whose heroism Steele contrasted with the false heroism of the pagans. The fourth endeavoured to show the value of religious motives to all men who aspire to greatness; and the conclusion was a tribute to a modern hero, William the Third. Such is the general design of the essay. The various strains of thought in it require a more detailed analysis.

Steele's view of human nature was on the whole

[1] *Dedication.*

[2] p. 68. The page numbers refer to the third edition, the pagination of which is indicated by marginal notations in the text of this edition.

[3] p. 4.

pessimistic. In the first place, natural depravity is fundamental. Pride and vanity caused the fall. Later, as social life grew more complex, the egoistic passions, 'Self-opinion' and 'Self-admiration', continued to become stronger, until 'from the desire of Superiority in our deprav'd Natures' there were bred 'Envy, Hatred, Cruelty, Cunning, Craft, and Debate' to be our 'bosom Companions'.[1] Thus egoism, a 'false and unreasonable Fondness of ourselves',[2] became firmly rooted in human nature.

A second point in Steele's analysis of human psychology was that the passions are 'the Springs of Human Action', whose important function it is to motivate conduct. But not all of them are evil. For example, love and the desire for fame, universal passions, are responsible for virtuous as well as evil actions. Revenge produces evil; but pity, an altruistic passion, produces highly virtuous conduct. Every action has its origin in a passion; and the passions are, therefore, the seeds of virtue as well as of vice. Although Steele's emphasis was on the primacy of the passions, he granted that reason is important as a check on them. But he lacked confidence in its power. 'The Living Conscience, or the Knowledge and Judgment of what we are doing'[3] was intended to be a guide. It has not sufficient power, however, to control the passions; and it cannot be trusted to define ethical standards. Steele's opinion was that

Whatever Law we may make to ourselves, from the Greatness of Nature or the Principles of Philosophy for the Conduct and Regulation of Life is it self but an Artificial Passion, by which we vainly hope to subdue those that are Natural.[4]

[1] pp. 33–4.   [2] p. 1.   [3] p. 74.   [4] p. 27.

Introduction

Thus human nature, weak in reason and ridden by passions, must have support and guidance. Christianity is effective, he believed, where pagan morality fails. It operates to save man, first through grace—that is, through the vicarious atonement by Christ, a mediator—and second through the precepts and examples of Christ and the early Christians. Christianity is able to control and direct the passions, to supply incentives of reward and punishment, and to define virtuous conduct. Steele emphasized the fact that it does not attempt to destroy the passions: God 'claims not an utter Extirpation, but the Direction only of our Passions'.[1] Accepting even the unruly ones as natural and useful, Christianity directs them into virtuous channels. Love is moralized by the Christian institution of marriage. Fame is given a wider scope—the undertaking of great deeds for the glory of God rather than for personal renown. And compassion, an altruistic passion, becomes the origin of charity, which is the supreme Christian duty, the 'reiterated Abridgment of all His Law'—the 'Command of Loving one another'. Thus Steele arrived at his criterion of virtue: that which contributes to 'The Good and Welfare of others'.[2] And he found that Christianity was superior to any other system of morality in its power to develop this social virtue:

> For the neglected and despised Tenets of Religion are so Generous, and in so Transcendent and Heroick a manner disposed for publick Good, that 'tis not in a Man's power to avoid their Influence; for the Christian is as much inclined to your Service when your Enemy, as the moral Man when your Friend.[3]

[1] p. 75.   [2] pp. 80–1.   [3] p. 85.

Introduction

But in spite of the fact that it was his lack of confidence in the rational faculty which caused him to advocate moral guidance by a system with supernatural sanctions, Steele made a special point of the approval of Christian doctrines by reason. Christ's teachings, he insisted, were directed to 'the Reason and Judgment' and must be received by '*Arduous* and *Indisputable Conviction*'.[1] Religious incentives are the 'reasonable terms of Reward and Punishment'. Saint Paul's preaching 'strikes all along at the Reason'.[2]

Steele's interest in reason, however, was perfunctory; his confidence in it, slight. Indeed one particular emphasis in his moral theory, as he outlined it in this essay, was its anti-rationalism. All men are moved primarily by passions, which are, in the main, egoistic; depravity and irrationality must be taken for granted. But Steele was unwilling to draw completely pessimistic conclusions. He saw nothing in human nature that precluded virtue—under the corrective influence of Christianity. And he declared that side by side with depravity is a natural 'Temper of Mind' hospitable to virtue; that by the 'Force of their Make' men are 'framed for mutual Kindness'.[3]

This idealism concerning man's innate tendency to good nature is one element in Steele's sentimentalism. But the sentimentalism in the *Christian Hero* lies chiefly in his conception of virtue, which he defined as Christian benevolence, insisting on its affinity with good nature, its origin in compassion, its association with humility, meekness, a forgiving spirit, and submission to the will of God, its amiability, and finally its appeal to the sensibilities. A pronounced

[1] p. 36.   [2] p. 50.   [3] pp. 80–1.

Introduction

fervour pervades his discussion of charity. Forgiveness is 'the most arduous Pitch human Nature can arrive at';[1] reconciliation with one's enemies, 'consummate Bliss';[2] meekness, a 'Sublime and Heroick Virtue'; pity, 'a beautiful kind of Ignorance' which men have of their own selfish affairs; charity, 'a noble Spark of Celestial Fire'.[3]

These three prominent emphases in Steele's moral theory—his anti-rationalistic analysis of human nature, his refusal to accept the pessimistic implications of such an analysis, and his sentimentality—are all related to the dominant intention of the essay, an attack on the claims of neo-Stoicism. Every element in his belief has anti-Stoic colouring. His disparagement of the reason as an ethical guide, his defence of the passions, his appeal to the sensibilities, and his insistence that morality must be Christian—all support the claim that his system is not a 'Stoical Rant'.[4]

III

The Stoic exaltation of reason had been revived at the end of the sixteenth century and the beginning of the seventeenth in the writings of Montaigne, Justus Lipsius, Du Vair, and Charron; it gradually permeated the ethical thought of the age and was still a potent force at the time Steele wrote.[5] Briefly, the tenets of neo-Stoicism relevant to the present

---

[1] p. 83. [2] p. 84. [3] p. 80. [4] p. 77.

[5] He quoted, for example, in the *Christian Hero* (p. 61) from L'Estrange's translation of Seneca. This translation (1678) had reached a fifth edition by 1693. The currency of neo-Stoic ideas is attested also by Charles Cotton's translation of Du Vair's *De la philosophie morale des stoïques* (1664); Nathaniel Wanley's translation of Justus Lipsius' *Discourse of Constancy* (1670); Ellis Walker's *Epicteti Enchiridion* (1692); and George Stanhope's *Epictetus His Morals with Simplicius His Comment* (1694 and 1700).

xviii   *Introduction*

discussion were as follows: Stoic philosophy furnishes reliable moral precepts and examples. The passions are not natural to man. They are all culpable. And as they are a hindrance to virtue, they should be exterminated. A miracle, however, is not needed to combat them, for reason is thoroughly adequate to the task. As Le Grand summed it up in his *Man without Passion or the Wise Stoick*:

> Reason is then Man's only benefit: he must use it to climbe heaven, he must consult it to govern his Life, and if he do but hearken unto her, he shall be vertuous, and tame the most insolent of his Passions.[1]

The moral ideal aimed at, then, was a 'man without passion', invincible to pleasure and pain, characterized by constancy and fortitude. Cato was usually praised as such a man.

The revival of Stoicism, however, provoked a vigorous reaction. Anti-Stoic propaganda, incidental in sermons, moral essays, and religious tracts, was clearly set forth in such treatises as Senault's *De l'usage des passions*, Timothy Nourse's *Nature and Faculties of Man*, and the adaptation of Senault's essay in 1700, by Captain Ayloffe, who apparently was a member of Steele's immediate social group.[2] The passions are natural, these moralists declared. Many of them, to be sure, are vicious; but all are potentially ethical. 'Passions are useful, and consistent with

---

[1] *Man without Passion or the Wise Stoick* (translated by G. R., 1675), p. 27.

[2] I have not seen a copy of Ayloffe's essay, *The Government of the Passions*. But a review of it in the *History of the Works of the Learned* (Jan. 1700), ii. 46 ff., indicates clearly its relation to Senault. Both Ayloffe and Steele seem to have been among the wits at Will's Coffee House against whom Richard Blackmore, in 1700, directed his *Satyr against Wit*. Steele retorted, with others, in *Commendatory Verses* (1700) edited by Tom Brown. Some of Ayloffe's writings were published in 1702 with those of Brown.

Introduction xix

human Nature in its highest Perfection,' says Nourse.[1] Morality consists not in stifling them but in moderating and regulating them: 'I dare say in their behalf, that there is none of them so despicable, but it may be changed into a Glorious Virtue.'[2] But the power of reason to regulate these passions had been overpraised by the Stoics. To judge by results, it had been clearly inadequate alone and must be assisted by religion. Again to quote Senault:

> To lead on successfully so glorious an enterprize, we must take a clean differing path from that of the Philosophers. ... for these blind men would have no other rule than Nature, no other help than Reason. ... But our malady was grown too great to be cured by such weak remedies; and it behoved, that Grace should be mingled with Nature, to make Vertue meritorious.[3]

Disapproval of the stock examples of Stoic morality was often expressed by these moralists. The wise man as drawn by Seneca and Epictetus was believed to be imaginary. Heathen virtues were branded as spurious. Cato's fortitude, for example, was only intolerable pride. As in the following passage, Cato was often singled out for disparaging comparison with the early Christians:

> Saint Paul and the Primitive Christians, had doubtless more Vertue than *Cato* and all the *Stoicks* ... Alas, poor Cato! thou fanciest thy Vertue raises thee above all things: whereas thy Wisdom is Folly, and thy magnanimity abominable before God; whatever the Wisemen of the World may think of it.[4]

---

[1] *Nature and Faculties of Man* (1686), pp. 105–6.
[2] Senault, *The Use of the Passions* (translated by Henry Earl of Monmouth, 1649), Preface.   [3] *Ibid.*
[4] *Father Malebranche's Treatise Concerning the Search after Truth* (translated by T. Taylor, 1694), Bk. II, Chap. iv, pp. 93–4.

Introduction

But the most prominent defect in the Stoic wise man, according to these moralists, was his lack of charity. Charity was the particular virtue claimed by them exclusively for Christians. The leading principle of Christianity, sympathy for others, was omitted from Stoic morality, because pity, the mainspring of charity, was a passion; and passions were not found in the wise man.

> We may not pity the miserable, as *Seneca* tells us, but he allows us to *help* him: But if we have not *compassion* our relief will be very *slow* and *slender* ...

was Richard Kidder's explanation.[1] Even the apologist for Stoicism, George Stanhope, admitted that were Stoic rules literally and strictly followed, 'Natural Affection and Charity among Men' would be destroyed. He commented with approval on the appeal of charity to the sensibilities: 'It inspires Compassion and Good Nature, and the tenderest Resentments of other People's Misfortunes.'[2] Praise of charity was not, of course, confined to religious writings in the anti-Stoic vein, but was to be found in the pages of such widely read writers as Jeremy Taylor, Sir Matthew Hale, Richard Allestree, John Scott, William Sherlock, Isaac Barrow, and John Tillotson.[3] And in their writings, as in Steele's

---

[1] *A Demonstration of the Messias* (written 1684–1700) (1726), Bk. I, p. 137.
[2] *Epictetus His Morals* (2nd ed., 1700), Preface.
[3] Tillotson (*Works*, 3 vols., 9th ed., 1700), Sermons on 'A New Commandment I Give Unto You', i. 169–76, and 'Of Doing Good', ii. 593–601; Richard Allestree, *Works of the Learned and Pious Author of the Whole Duty of Man* (Oxford, 1704), pp. 126 ff.; Henry Waring, *The Rule of Charity* (1701); Jacques Abbadie, *L'esprit du Christianisme ou l'excellence de la charité* (1694); William Sherlock, *The Nature and Measure of Charity* (1697); Edward Pelling, *A Practical Discourse upon Charity* (1693); Isaac Barrow (*Works*, 3 vols., 1700), Sermons on 'The Nature, Properties, and Acts of Charity', 'Motives and Arguments to

Introduction

Christian Hero, the personal virtue of Christian charity was definitely related to the larger social ideal of benevolence. One quotation will serve to indicate the tenor of all:

> This Religion teaches us to prefer the *publick good* before our *private*, to prefer what is *just* to what we judge *commodious*, to abridge our selves of our *own* liberties for the good of others.[1]

Other forces at work in the seventeenth century likewise served to counterbalance the Stoic propaganda. It is not necessary to pause on Augustinian theology, never stronger than in seventeenth-century Puritanism with its stress on the irrationality and depravity of man and on the consequent need of salvation by grace. And reason—as well as religion—was in complete disrepute with the group of moralists whose anti-rationalistic analysis of human nature was expounded by La Rochefoucauld in France and by Hobbes in England. These moralists believed in the complete tyranny of the selfish passions over reason. They regarded man as psychologically incapable of rational thought and action. He is so completely possessed with pride and self-love that he has not the ability even to listen to the dictates of reason: 'L'esprit est toujours la dupe du cœur' declared La Rochefoucauld.[2] Pierre Bayle,

---

Charity', 'The Duty and Reward of Bounty to the Poor', 'Of the Love of our Neighbor', 'Impiety and Impotence of Paganism and Mahometanism'; George Stanhope, *A Sermon on Christian Charity* (1701).

It is interesting and doubtless significant that Steele's chapter on charity in the *Ladies' Library* (1714) is made up of excerpts from discussions of charity by Taylor, Scott, and Allestree.

[1] Richard Kidder, *op. cit.*, p. 152.
[2] *Réflexions ou sentences et maximes morales* (1664–5) (ed. Gilbert, Paris, 1868), i. cii.

another arch-sceptic, saw in the furious war between reason and the passions no possibility of morality, for reason is both 'juge et partie, et ses arrêts ne sont point exécutés'.[1] Hobbes demonstrated in the *Leviathan* (1651) that the concept of duty cannot possibly originate elsewhere than in the passions of desire or aversion and that the reason is merely 'the last appetite in deliberating'.[2] As for his criterion of good and evil:

> Whatever is the object of any man's appetite or desire, that is it which he for his part calleth *good*: and the object of his hate and aversion, *evil*.[3]

Thus the impotency of reason and the selfishness of the passions were arraigned as beyond remedy, and virtuous conduct was declared impossible under the guidance of Christianity or any other moral system.[4]

To many moralists who found no attractions in neo-Stoicism, these forms of anti-rationalism seemed even more objectionable. All Christian moralists would naturally disapprove of extremists who considered the irrationality of human nature to be beyond even the aid of religion. The Latitudinarians of the Anglican Church were uneasy also at the variance of anti-rationalistic theology from the dominant note of the age. They attempted, therefore, to give reason more prestige in the realm of religion. Joseph Glanvill, an early liberal, warned against 'the

---

[1] *Dictionnaire historique et critique* (1697), art. on *Ovide*, note H.
[2] *Leviathan*, Part I, Chap. vi; *Works*, iii. 49.
[3] *Ibid.*, p. 49.
[4] For a thorough survey of this current of thought, see F. B. Kaye, '*Fable of the Bees*', *by Bernard Mandeville* (Oxford, 1924), I. lxxvi–cxiv.

dangerous tendency of declaiming against Reason as an Enemy to Religion'.[1] There should not be an

> unnatural divorce between the Wise and the Good. These conceiving Reason and Philosophy sufficient vouchees of Licentious practices and their secret scorn of Religion; and Those reckoning it a great instance of Piety and devout Zeal, vehemently to declaim against Reason and Philosophy ... That 'Tis a piece of Wit and Gallantry to be an Atheist, and of Atheism to be a Philosopher.[2]

Omitting reason from faith puts religion out of countenance with philosophers and leaves it to the mercy of 'Enthusiastic Spirits'.[3] Hence, while such liberals as Tillotson, Sherlock, and South agreed with the prevailing religious view as to the insufficiency of reason as a moral guide, they pointed out that it performs the highly important function of proving revealed religion and its supernatural sanctions. The 'reasonableness' of religion was a constantly recurring subject. John Locke's exposition of the theme in his *Reasonableness of Christianity* (1695) was typical of many discussions.

Undoubtedly the cynicism in the egoistic theory of human nature, which denied the possibility of virtue, intensified belief in the innate beneficence of man. A trend of thought opposed to the anti-rationalistic analysis described 'good nature' as an inherent quality and love for humanity as a more powerful passion than self-love. A tendency towards altruism, as Isaac Barrow expressed it, was 'planted in our original constitution by the breath of God'.[4]

---

[1] 'Agreement of Reason and Religion' in *Essays on Several Important Subjects in Philosophy and Religion* (1676), p. 24.
[2] *Scepsis Scientifica or Confest Ignorance* (1665), Dedication.
[3] *Ibid.* [4] *Works* (1700), i. 305.

xxiv   *Introduction*

'The frame of our Nature disposeth us to it' according to Tillotson.[1] Such views had wide currency. They were expressed not only in the pages of the Cambridge Platonists, More and Whichcote, but also in the sermons of Tillotson, South, Beveridge, Sherlock, and Barrow; in Rapin, Fénelon, and Malebranche, and in the latter's English disciple, John Norris; and in the tracts of Henry Waring, Jeremy Collier, and Edward Pelling. Panegyrics of human nature were often explicitly directed against Hobbes' theories and were always associated with discussions of the Christian virtue, charity. Barrow found it

> a monstrous paradox, crossing the common sense of men, which in this loose and vain world hath lately got such vogue, that all men naturally are enemies one to another. . . . All men are friends and disposed to entertain friendly correspondence with one another.[2]

Tillotson declared in his sermon on *Loving our Enemies* that

> So far is it from being true, which Mr. Hobbes asserts as the fundamental Principle of his Politicks, that Men are naturally in a State of War and Enmity with one Another; that the contrary Principle . . . is most certainly true, that Men are naturally a-kin and Friends to each other.[3]

The beauty and amiability of charity, meekness, and a forgiving spirit inspired passages pervaded by emotional ecstasy. Beveridge defined charity as 'the bond of perfectness that perfectly ties all men together'.[4] Waring insisted that 'our charity should be moistened with tears of Pity'—that 'the Sluices of Grief should

[1] *Works* (9th ed., 1728), i. 171.   [2] *Works* (1700), i. 339.
[3] *Works* (9th ed., 1728), i. 176.   [4] *Works* (Oxford, 1818), vi. 132.

Introduction

remain open, to render the Charity Perfect'.[1] Scott urged that 'this blessed Disposition of Universal Charity' was intended to prepare men for heavenly society.[2] Barrow, who found in charity 'a beauty and majesty apt to ravish every heart', recommended to all men 'the practice of benignity, of courtesy, of clemency as acceptable and amiable to their mind, as beauty to their sight, harmony to their hearing, fragrancy to their smell, and sweetness to their taste'.[3]

IV

It was under the pressure of these conflicting points of view that Steele's ideas were formed. His central theme, 'No principles but those of religion are sufficient to make a great man,' expressed disapproval of the claims of neo-Stoicism that reason is a trustworthy moral guide and that pagan precepts and examples constitute an adequate moral system. Such a system was ineffective, he insisted with other Christian moralists, because of man's natural depravity—his impotent reason and selfish passions. This analysis of human nature agreed, of course, with the views of anti-Stoic moralists; it was supported by Augustinian theology; and up to a certain point, it harmonized with the egoistic theory.

Steele, however, did not accept the gloom of Augustinian theology or the cynicism of the egoistic analysis. The first element in his optimism was his confidence, shared with many anti-Stoic moralists, in the passions as natural—hence defensible—and manageable. The Stoic doctrine of insensibility was

[1] *The Rule of Charity* (1690), pp. 4–5.
[2] *The Christian Life* (1681), p. 187.
[3] *Works* (1700), i. 339.

as distasteful to him as it was to his fellow moralists. He regarded the Stoic wise man, governed entirely by reason, without sensibilities, and invincible to pleasure and pain, not only as an unattainable human ideal but also as an undesirable one. The passions were to be defended as the springs of action; benevolence itself sprang from pity. Steele also found cause for optimism, as did others who disapproved of the egoistic theory, in a strong belief that human nature has a natural inclination towards benevolence. And finally, he was completely confident of the power of revealed religion. With the Augustinians, he relied on the saving element of grace and the invaluable check on depravity of reward and punishment. With the anti-Stoic moralists he believed religion capable of giving ethical direction to the passions. The reasonableness of Christianity, which the Latitudinarians stressed, he believed was also in its favour. And with all Christian moralists, he insisted that benevolence, the supreme virtue, is in its origin and nature peculiarly Christian. However seemingly inconsistent were his views, they were unified by his belief that Christianity, and no other moral system, will ensure right conduct.

Thus altruism and egoism, rationalism and anti-rationalism, natural and supernatural sanctions were intermingled in Steele's thought. But such contradictions were not peculiar to him. It is obvious that they existed also in the doctrines of contemporary Christian moralists who, like Steele, sensed danger both in the exaltation and in the denial of reason. The effort to combat in one synthesis both of these dangerous extremes accounts for the fact that in their

Introduction

doctrines, side by side with an element of pessimism conceding man's irrationality and depravity, there was an element of idealism praising his natural goodness. One fact should be emphasized: the strain of idealism in Steele's moral theory was not completely flattering to human nature—his was not a facile optimism.

The *Christian Hero* did not make any important new contribution to the ethical thought of the age. Steele's ideas were all ideas widely diffused among his contemporaries. There is no new single element in his essay and nothing original in his synthesis. And in fairness, it should be said that others writing in a similar vein—Abbadie, Nourse, and Malebranche—set forth their position much more thoroughly and clearly than Steele did. His essay, however, is more appealing. The reader turns gratefully from seventeenth-century sermons, reforming tracts, moral essays, and manuals of piety to the *Christian Hero*, which has, in addition to the earnestness characterizing them all, an appealing generosity of spirit and persuasive grace.

The principles which Steele laid down in the *Christian Hero* he adhered to, in the main, in his later reforming designs. As Isaac Bickerstaff and the Spectator, addressing a larger social group, he still regarded it as the chief duty of the moralist 'to look out for some Expedient to turn the Passions and Affections on the Side of Truth and Honor'.[1] Religion he continued to praise as the most noble expedient—'the most honourable Incentive to good and worthy Actions'.[2] And he continued to urge

[1] *Spectator*, No. 394.   [2] *Spectator*, No. 356.

xxviii *Introduction*

upon the fine gentleman the compatibility of religion and good breeding. The 'Word Christian', the Spectator admonished, should carry with it 'All that is Great, Worthy, Friendly, Generous, and Heroick'.[1] The Guardian reaffirmed the purpose of Captain Steele:

> However, I will not despair but to bring men of wit into a love and admiration of the Sacred Writings; and, old as I am, I promise myself to see the day when it shall be as much in fashion among men of politeness to admire a rapture of Saint Paul, as any fine expression in Virgil or Horace; and to see a well-dressed young man produce an evangelist out of his pocket, and be no more out of countenance than if it were a classic printed by Elzevir.[2]

Nevertheless it is apparent that, as the years passed, Steele's ideas about what could and what should motivate right conduct came to be modified, probably as a result of the insistence of many of his contemporaries that the reason can furnish a basis for a moral life. He increasingly emphasized the nobility of rational motives—'conscious virtue' and 'conscious goodness'.[3] And unlike the Christian hero, his last hero, Bevil Junior of the *Conscious Lovers*, is first of all a rational being, whose 'actions are the result of thinking', who believes that 'there is nothing manly but what is conducted by reason'.[4]

In his mature writings, as in this first essay, Steele exalted benevolence as the supreme virtue. At the centre of all of his corrective propaganda was the principle that 'the good of others' is the 'most

---
[1] *Spectator*, No. 356. [2] *Guardian*, No. 21.
[3] See *Tatler*, Nos. 13 and 76; *Spectator*, No. 346; *Englishman*, No. 10; *Lover*, No. 8; *Theatre*, No. 13; *Conscious Lovers*, ii. 2.
[4] ii. 2 and iv. 1.

Introduction

generous motive of life'.[1] He continued to identify benevolence with the Christian virtue, charity. And as an extract from a famous political pamphlet written at the height of his career will serve to indicate, his discussions of this virtue were pervaded by an emotional fervour similar to the sentimentalism of the *Christian Hero*:

... tho I may be ridiculous for saying it, I hope I am animated in my Conduct by a Grace which is as little practised as understood, and that is Charity. ... The greatest Merit is in having social Virtues, such as Justice and Truth exalted with Benevolence to Mankind. ... He who has warmed his Heart with Impressions of this kind, will find Glowings of Good-will, which will Support him in the Service of his Country against all Calumny, Reproach and Invective, that can be thrown upon him. Riches and Honours can administer to the Heart no Pleasure, like what an Honest Man feels when he is contending for the Interest of his Country, and the Civil Rights of his Fellow-Subjects.[2]

---

[1] *Tatler*, No. 183.
[2] *The Importance of Dunkirk Considered* (1713), pp. 57–8.

A NOTE ON THE TEXT

A COMPLETE collation of the eight numbered editions of the *Christian Hero* published by Tonson during Steele's lifetime (the Dublin edition, 1725, has not been included in this collation) yields unmistakable evidence that the third edition, published in November 1710, contains Steele's final revisions. It is taken, consequently, as the basis of this edition.

The first edition, published in April, 1701, was followed in July of the same year by a second, revised and considerably enlarged. Both were carelessly printed, however, the second containing several of the misprints of the first edition as well as many new ones. The third edition, published nine years later, was printed from a copy of the second, which had been subjected by both the compositor and Steele to a thorough overhauling. The uniform arrangement and italicizing of the quotations, the additional punctuation—in the main helpful—the more consistent use of capitals, the standardizing of the spelling, and the correction of obvious printer's errors are probably attributable to the compositor. But Steele's hand is clearly seen in more than sixty careful stylistic alterations, such as expansion of hasty or colloquial expressions, corrections of redundancies, deletions, substitutions in diction, and rearrangement of phrases and clauses.

Subsequent editions published before Steele's death (1729) retained the text of the third edition unchanged except for such minor variations as the correction of its misprints and the accumulation of new ones. The fourth edition was printed from the third, the fifth from the fourth, the sixth from the fifth, and the seventh from the sixth. The eighth and last in his life was apparently printed from the third. This relationship is indicated by the fact that in such details as spelling, punctuation, and capitalization, the eighth agrees with the third much more frequently than with the other four editions. Also, misprints occurring in the third but corrected in the fourth, fifth, sixth, and seventh are retained in the eighth;[1] and misprints peculiar to the fourth, fifth, sixth, and seventh are not shared by the eighth, which resembles the third.[2] This reversion

[1] For example, *tasts*, 3rd and 8th, is correctly printed *tastes*, 4th–7th (see 3rd ed., p. 29); *do's*, 3rd and 8th, is correctly printed *does*, 4th–7th (see 3rd ed., p. 57).

[2] For example, *these*, 3rd and 8th, is misprinted *these two*, 4th–7th (see 3rd ed., Preface); *of it*, 3rd and 8th, is misprinted *to it*, 4th–7th (see 3rd ed., p. 73).

to the third may be regarded, perhaps, as an additional reason for accepting it as definitive.[1]

The present edition is, therefore, a reproduction of a copy of the third,[2] with no changes whatever except the correction of a few verbal misprints. These corrections are all made in the light of the readings in the first edition. Only significant variants are recorded. Variants regarded as significant are those for which Steele must have been responsible, that is, verbal alterations involving the addition, deletion, substitution, and rearrangement of words. These comprise the stylistic differences between the first and second editions and the enlargement of the text in the second edition. No record is made of the many variations in spelling, punctuation, italics, capitals, arrangement of quoted passages, and placing of reference notes, as it is not likely that responsibility for them rests with Steele.

The three editions referred to in the textual notes—(1) 1701, (2) 1701, and (3) 1710—are designated as *01*[1], *01*[2], and *10*. The abbreviation *add.* means that the passage referred to was added to the text at the date given in the note. The pagination of the third edition is indicated by marginal notations.

[1] The French translation, 1727 (see Bibliography), is based on a text subsequent to that of the second edition—which one it is impossible to determine.

[2] This copy, which is in the University of Chicago Library, is described in the Bibliography.

PREFACE

THE World is divided between two sorts of People, the Men of Wit and the Men of Business, and these[1] have it wholly in their Power; but however Mighty the latter may esteem themselves, they have much the less share in the Government of Mankind, and till they can keep the others out of Company as well as Employment, they will have an almost Irresistible Dominion over us: For their Imagination is so very quick and lively, that in all they enjoy or possess, they have a Relish highly Superior to that of slower Men; which fine Sense of things they can communicate to others in so prevailing a manner, that they give and take away what Impressions they please; for while the Man of Wit speaks, he bestows upon his Hearers, by an apt Representation of his Thoughts, all the Happiness and Pleasure of being such as he is, and quickens our heavier Life into Joys we should never of our selves have tasted, so that we are for our own sakes his Slaves and Followers: But indeed they generally use this charming Force with the utmost Tyranny, and as 'tis too much in their Power, misplace our Love, our Hatred, our Desires and Aversions, on improper Objects; so that when we are left to our selves, we find Truth discolour'd to us, and they of Faculties above us have wrapt things, in their own nature of a dark and horrid Aspect, in so bright a Disguise, that they have stamp'd a kind of Praise and Gallantry

[1] See 'A Note on the Text', p. xxxi, n. 2.

on some Vices, and[a] half persuaded us that a Whore may be still a Beauty, and an Adulterer no Villain.

These Ills are supported by the Arbitrary Sway of Legislative Ridicule, while by, I know not what Pedantry of good Breeding, Conversation is confin'd to Indifferent, Low, or perhaps Vitious Subjects; and all that is Serious, Good or Great, almost Banished the World: For in Imitation of those we have mentioned, there daily arise so many Pretenders to do Mischief, that what seem'd at first but a Conspiracy, is now a general Insurrection against Virtue; and when they who really have Wit lead the way it is hardly to be prevented, but that they must be followed by a Crowd who would be such, and make what shift they can to appear so, by helping one Defect with another, and supplying want of Wit with want of Grace, and want of Reputation with want of Shame.

Thus are Men hurry'd away in the Prosecution of mean and sensual Desires, and instead of Employing their Passions in the service of Life, they spend their Life in the service of their Passions; yet tho' 'tis a Truth very little receiv'd, that Virtue is its own Reward, 'tis surely an undeniable one, that Vice is its own Punishment; for when we have giv'n our Appetites a loose Rein, we are immediately præcipitated by 'em into unbounded and endless Wishes, while we repine at our Fortune, if its Narrowness curbs 'em, tho' the Gratification of 'em were a Kindness, like the Indulgence of a Man's Thirst in a Dropsy; but this Distemper of Mind is never to be remedied, till Men will more unreservedly attempt

[a] stamp'd a Kind of praise and Gallantry on some Vices and *add. or*[2]

Preface

the Work, and will resolve to value themselves rather upon a strong Reason to allay their Passions, than a fine Imagination to raise 'em.

For if we best Judge of things when we are not actually engag'd or concern'd in 'em, every Man's own Experience must inform him, that both the Pleasures we follow, and the Sorrows we shun, are in Nature very different from what we conceive 'em, when we observe that past Enjoyments are Anxious, past Sufferings pleasing in the Reflection; and since the Memory of the one makes us apprehend our Strength, the other our Weakness, it is an Argument of a trivial Mind to prefer the Satisfactions that lead to Inquietude before Pains that lead to Tranquility.

But if that consists (as it certainly does) in the Mind's enjoyment of Truth, the most vexatious Circumstance of its Anguish, is that of being in Doubt; from which Men will find but a very short Relief, if they draw it from the Collections or Observations of sedentary Men, who have been call'd Wise for proposing Rules of active Life, which they cannot be supposed to understand: For between the Arrogant and Fanatick Indolence of some, and the false and pleasurable Felicity of others (which are equally Chimæras[a]) a Man is so utterly divided, that the Happiness of Philosophers appears as Fantastick as the Misery of Lovers.

We shall not, 'tis hop'd, be understood by saying this, to Imagine that there is a sufficient Force in the short following Essay[b], to stem the Universal and Destructive Torrent of Error and Pleasure; it is

[a] *Misprinted* Chimæra's *10*   [b] discourse *o1*[1]

sufficient if we can stand without being carry'd away with it, and we shall very willingly resign the Glory of an Opposition, if we can enjoy the Safety of a Defence; and as it was at first attempted to disengage my own Mind from deceiving Appearances, so it can be publish'd for no other end, but to set others a thinking with the same Inclination: Which whoever will please to do, will make a much better Argument for his own private Use, than any body else can for Him: For ill Habits of the Mind, no more than those of the Body,[a] are to be cur'd by the Patient's Approbation of the Medicine, except He'll resolve to take it; and if my Fellow-Soldiers (to whose Service more especially I would direct any Thoughts I were capable of) would form to themselves, (if any do not) a constant Reason of their Actions, they would find themselves better prepar'd for all the Vicissitudes they are to meet with, when instead of the Changeable Heat of mere Courage and Blood, they acted upon the firm Motives of Duty, Valour, and Constancy of Soul.

For (however they are dis-esteem'd by some Unthinking, not to say, Ungrateful Men) to Profess Arms, is to Profess being ready to Die for others; nor is it an Ordinary Struggle between Reason, Sense, and Passion, that can raise Men to a calm and ready Negligence of Life, and animate 'em to Assault without Fear, Pursue without Cruelty, and Stab without Hatred.[b]

But Virtuous Principles must infallibly be not only

[a] For ill Habits of the Mind, no more than those of the Body,] For Intellectual ill habits no more than Physical *01*[1]

[b] *This paragraph* 'For (however they are dis-esteem'd . . . Stab without Hatred.' *add. 01*[2]

Preface

better than any other We can Embrace, to Warm us to great Attempts,[a] but also to make Our Days in their Ordinary Passage slide away Agreeably: For as nothing is more daring than Truth, so there is nothing more Chearful than Innocence;[b] and indeed I need not have been beholden to the Experience of a various Life to have been convinc'd, that true Happiness is not to be found but where I at present place it;[c] For I was long ago inform'd where only it was to be had,[d] by the Reverend Dr. Ellis, my ever Honour'd Tutor; which Great Obligation I could not but Mention, tho' my Gratitude to Him is perhaps an Accusation of my self, who shall appear to have so little Profited by the Institution of so Solid and Excellent a Writer, tho' he is above the Temptation of (what is always in his Power) being Famous.[1]

---

[a] But Virtuous Principles . . . to Warm us to great Attempts,] And such Principles must infallibly be better than any other we can Embrace, not only to warm us to great Attempts, *o1*

[b] For as nothing . . . than Innocence;] For what can be thought more daring than Truth, more chearful than Innocence: *o1*

[c] Happiness is not . . . place it;] Happiness is only to be found where I at present place it. *o1*

[d] inform'd where only it was to be had,] told where only I should find it *o1*

---

[1] Dr. Welbore Ellis, who was also chaplain of the regiment in which Steele first served, the Second Troop of Guards. See G. A. Aitken, *Life of Richard Steele*, i. 32.

The Christian Hero:
OR,
No Principles but those of
RELIGION
SUFFICIENT
To make a Great Man.

IT is certainly the most useful Task we can possibly Undertake, to rescue our Minds from the Prejudice with which a false and unreasonable Fondness of our selves has enslaved us. But the Examination of our own Bosoms is so ungrateful an Exercise, that we are forc'd upon a Thousand little Arts, to lull our Selves into an imperfect Tranquility, which we might obtain sincere and uninterrupted, if we had Courage enough to look at the ghastly Part of our Condition: But we are still | Flatterers to our selves, and Hypocrites the wrong way, by chusing, instead of the solid Satisfaction of Innocence and Truth, the returning Pangs of Conscience, and working out our Damnation as we are taught to do our Happiness, *with Fear and Trembling*.

But this Misfortune we owe, as we do most others, to an unjust Education, by which we are inspir'd with an Ambition of acquiring such Modes and Accomplishments, as rather enable us to give Pleasure and Entertainment to others, than Satisfaction and Quiet to our selves: So Phantastical are we as to dress for a Ball when we are to set out on a Journey, and upon Change of Weather, are justly derided, not pitied by the Beholders. How then shall we prepare for the unaccountable Road of Life, when we know not how long or how short it will prove, or what Accidents we shall meet in our Passage? Can we take any thing with us that can make us chearful, ready and prepar'd for all Occasions, and can support us against all Encounters? Yes, we may (if we would receive it) a Confidence in God. Yet, lest this be impos'd upon Men by a blind force of Custom, or the Artifice of such Persons whose Interest perhaps it may be to obtrude upon our Mirth, and our Gaiety, and give us a melancholy Prospect[a] (as some Men would persuade us)[b] to maintain themselves in the Luxury they deny us; let us not be frighted from the liberal use of our Senses, or meanly resign our present Opinions, 'till we are convinc'd from our own Reflection also, that there is something in that Opinion which can make us less insolent in Joy, less depress'd in Adversity, than the Methods we are already engag'd[c] in. And indeed the chief Cause of Irresolution in either State, must proceed from the want of an adæquate Motive to our Actions, that can render Men Dauntless and Invincible both to Pleasure and Pain.

It were not then, methinks, an useless Enquiry to search into the Reason that we are so willing to arm our selves against the Assaults of Delight and Sorrow, rather with the Dictates of Morality than those of Religion; and how it has obtain'd, that when we say a thing was done like an old *Roman*, we have a

[a] a melancholy Prospect] Melancholy prospects *o1*[1]
[b] (as some men would persuade Us) *add. o1*[2]
[c] engag'd *add. o1*[2]

The Christian Hero

generous and sublime Idea, that warms and kindles in us, together with a certain Self-disdain, a desire of Imitation; when, on the other side, to say, 'twas like a Primitive Christian, chills Ambition, and seldom rises to more than the cold approbation of a Duty that perhaps a Man wishes he were not oblig'd to. Or, in a word, why is it that the Heathen struts, and the Christian sneaks in our Imagination: If it be as *Machiavil* says, that Religion throws our Minds below | noble and hazardous Pursuits, then its Followers are Slaves and Cowards; but if it gives a more hardy and aspiring Genius than the World before knew, then He, and All our fine Observers, who have been pleas'd to give us only Heathen Portraitures, to say no worse, have robb'd their Pens of Characters the most truly Gallant and Heroick that ever appear'd to Mankind.

About the time the World receiv'd the best News it ever heard, The Men whose Actions and Fortunes are most pompously array'd in Story, had just acted or were then performing their Parts, as if it had been the Design of Providence to prepossess at that time, after a more singular manner than ordinary, the Minds of Men, with the Trappings and Furniture of Glory and Riches, to heighten the Virtue and Magnanimity of those who were to oppose 'em all, by passing through Wants, Miseries and Disgraces; and indeed the shining Actions of these illustrious Men do yet glare so much in our Faces, that we lose our Way by following a false Fire, which well consider'd is but a delusive Vapour of the Earth, when we might enjoy the leading constant Light of Heav'n.

To make therefore a just Judgment in our Con-

duct, let us consider two or three of the most eminent
[5] Heathen, and observe whether | they, or we, are
better appointed for the hard and weary March of
human Life; for which Examination we will not look
into the Closets of Men of Reflection and Retire-
ment, but into the Practice and Resolution of those
of Action and Enterprize. There were never Persons
more conspicuously of this latter sort, than those concern'd in the Fortunes and Death of *Cæsar*; and since
the Pulse of Man then beat at the highest, we will
think it sufficient to our Purpose carefully to review
Him, and Them, as they March by us, and if we can
see any apparent Defect in their Armour, find out
some way to mend it in our own. But it will require
all our Patience, by taking notice of the minutest
Things, to come at (what is absolutely necessary to
us) the Recesses of their Hearts, and Folds of their
Tempers.

Sallust has transmitted to us two very great, but
very different Personages, *Cæsar* and *Cato*, and plac'd
them together in the most judicious Manner for
appearing to advantage, by the alternate Light and
Shade of each other: *Cæsar*'s Bounty, Magnificence,
Popular and Sumptuous Entertainments stole an
universal Affection; *Cato*'s Parsimony, Integrity,
Austere and Rigid Behaviour commanded as universal Reverence: None could do an ungentile thing
[6] before *Cæsar*, none a loose one before *Cato*: | To one
'twas Recommendation enough to be Miserable, to
the other to be Good: To *Cæsar* all Faults were par-
donable, to *Cato* none: One gave, oblig'd, pity'd and
succour'd indifferently; t'other blam'd, oppos'd, and
condemn'd impartially: *Cæsar* was the Refuge of the

Unhappy, *Cato* the Bane of the Wicked: *Cato* had rather be, than seem Good; *Cæsar* was careless of either, but as it serv'd his Interests: *Cato*'s Sword was the Sword of Justice, *Cæsar*'s that of Ambition: *Cæsar* had an excellent common Sense and right Judgment of Occasion, Time and Place; the other blunt Man understood not Application, knew how to be in the Right, but was generally so, out of Season: *Cæsar*'s Manner made even his Vice charming, *Cato*'s even[a] his Virtue disagreeable: *Cæsar* insinuated Ill, *Cato* intruded Good: *Cæsar* in his Sayings, his Actions and his Writings was the first and happiest of all Men: In his Discourse he had a constant Wit and right Reason; in his Actions, Gallantry and Success; in his Writings, every thing that any Author can pretend to, and one which perhaps no Man else ever had; he mentions himself with a good Grace. Thus it was very natural for *Cæsar*, adorn'd with every Art, Master of every necessary Quality, either for Use or Ornament, with a steady and well-plac'd | Industry [7] to out-run *Cato*, and all like him, who had none and desir'd none, but (an ever weak Party) the Good for his Friends.

Now this sort of Men were *Cæsar* and *Cato*, and by these Arts they arriv'd[b] at that height, which has left one's Name proverbial for a Noble and Princely Nature, t'other's for an Unmov'd and Inexorable Honesty: Yet, without following 'em thro' all the handsome Incidents and Passages of Life, we may know 'em well enough in Miniature, by beholding 'em only in their manner of Dying: For in those last Minutes, the Soul and Body both collect all their

---

[a] even *add. 01²* [b] they arriv'd] arriv'd they *01¹*

Force, either bravely to oppose the Enemy, or gracefully receive the *Conqueror*, Death.

Cæsar, by a long Tract of Successes, was now become apparent Master of his Country, but with a Security, that's natural to gallant Men, Heroically forgave the most inveterate of his Opposers: Now was He follow'd with Applause, Renown, and Acclamation: His Valour had subdued the Bodies, his Clemency the Minds of his Enemies: And how bless'd must the Earth be under his Command, who seems to court Dominion for no other end, but to indulge an insatiable Mind in the glorious Pleasures of bestowing and forgiving? This was the Figure *Cæsar* bore in the World's Opinion, | but not in *Cato*'s. He was there a Tyrant in spite of the Gloss of Success and of Fortune, which could not create Appearances bright enough to dazzle his Eyes from seeing the Traitor in the Conqueror: He knew to give a Man his own as a Bounty was but a more impudent Robbery, and a Wrong improv'd by the Slavery of an Obligation: He justly and generously disdain'd that his Fellow Citizen shou'd pretend to be his Lord; to his honest Mind a Pardon was but a more arrogant Insult, nor could he bear the Apprehension of seeing his Equal inflict upon him a *tyrannical Forgiveness*: What then must this unhappy good Man do? Whither shall oppress'd Virtue fly from Slavery? From *Slavery*? *No*. He is still Free Lord of Himself, and Master of his Passions; *Cæsar* is the Captive, He is Shackl'd, He is Chain'd, and the numerous Troops which he boasts the Companions of his Triumphs, and his Glories, are but so many Witnesses of his Shame and Confusion, to whom he

The Christian Hero

has by an open Usurpation manifested his broken Faith, false Profession, and prostituted Honour. But how far this Impression of intrinsick Glory and Happiness in sincere, tho' distress'd Virtue, and the sense of a wicked Man's abject, tho' prosperous Condition (which *Cato*'s Philosophy gave Him) did avail in his afflicted Hours; the Resolution he is going to take will demonstrate. |

He had now at *Utica* fresh and shocking Intelligence of the gathering Adherents to his Enemy, and could read, in his own Company, the mere Followers of Fortune in their Countenance, but observ'd it with a negligent and undaunted Air, concern'd only for the Fate of others, whose weak Pity of themselves made 'em the Objects of his Compassion also. It was visible by a thousand little officious things he did, he was resolv'd to leave this bad World: For he spent the Day, which he design'd should be his last,[a] in a certain Vanity of Goodness: He Consulted, Persuaded, and Dispatch'd all he thought necessary for the Safety of those that were about him; which Services they receiv'd from him, whose Intent they saw, with Tears, and Shame, and Admiration.

He continued the whole Evening this affected Enjoyment of his Friends Anxiety for him, which he rais'd by set Discourses, and abated, or rather confirm'd by a studied Indifference, 'till he went to Bed, where he read *Plato*'s Immortality, and Guesses at a future Life: At last he enquir'd for his Sword, on purpose mis-laid by his Son; they did not immediately bring it, which he seem'd to take no notice of, but again fell to his Book: After his Second

---

[a] which he design'd should be his last,] he design'd his last, *01¹, 01²*

Lecture, he again wanted his Sword: Their Hesitation in letting him have it, threw him into an unseemly Rage, and Expostulation with his Friends, whose obliging Sorrow with-held it: What has he done, what has he committed, to be betray'd into the Hands of his Enemy? Had *Cato*'s Wisdom so far left him, that he must be disarm'd, like a Slave and a Madman? What had his Son seen so indiscreet in his Father, that he was not to be trusted with himself? To all this cruel and intemperate Question, he was answer'd with the humblest Behaviour, tenderest Beseeching, and deepest Esteem; They implor'd his Stay amongst 'em as their Genius, their Guardian, and Benefactor; Among the rest, a fond Slave was putting in his Resistance, and his Affliction, for which he dash'd the poor Fellow's Teeth out with his Fist, and forc'd out of the Room his lamenting Friends, with Noise, and Taunt, and Tumult; a little while after had his Hand with which he struck his Servant dress'd, lay down, and was heard to Snore; but sure we may charitably enough believe, from all this unquiet Carriage, that the Sleep was dissembled, from which as soon as he awak'd, he Stabb'd himself, and fell on the Floor; His Fall alarm'd his wretched Dependants, whose help he resisted by tearing open his own Bowels, and rushing out of Life with Fury, Rage, and Indignation. |

[11] This was the applauded Exit of that Noble *Roman*, who is said with a superior and invincible Constancy to have eluded the Partiality of Fortune, and escap'd the Incursion upon the Liberty of his Country: It seems then, had he liv'd, his own had been lost, and his calling himself still Free, and *Cæsar* the Usurper,

The Christian Hero

a Bond-man and Slave, were but mere Words; for his Opinion of things was in reality Stunn'd by Success, and he dy'd Disappointed of the Imaginary Self-Existence his own Set of Thoughts had promis'd him, by an Action below the Precepts of his Philosophy, and the Constancy of his Life.

Thus did *Cato* leave the World, for which indeed he was very unfit, in the Hands of the most Skilful Man in it, who at his entrance on its Empire excell'd his past Glorious Life, by using with so much Temper and Moderation what he had purchas'd with so much Bloodshed and Violence: But we must leave, at present, this busie and *Incessant* Mind to the Meditation of Levelling inaccessible Mountains, Checking the Course of the Ocean,[a] and correcting the Periods of Time: We must leave him employ'd in Modeling the Universe (now his own) in the secure Enjoyment of a Life hitherto led in Illustrious Hazards, and now every way | safe, but where 'tis its Beauty to lye open, to the Treachery of his Friends.

Among the many Pretenders to that Character was *Cassius*, an able and experienc'd Soldier, bound to him by no less an Obligation, than the giving him Life and Quarter in Battel; He was of a Dark, Sullen and *Involv'd* Spirit, quick to receive, but slow to discover a Distaste; His Anger never flew into his Face, but descended to his Heart, which rankled, and prey'd upon it self, and could not admit[b] of Composure, either from Religion or Philosophy; but being a perfect *Epicurean*, and fancying there were none, or if any, only Lazy and Supine Deities, must necessarily Terminate his Hopes and Fears in himself,

[a] the Ocean,] Oceans, *o1*¹ [b] admit] easily admit *o1*¹

and from his own Arm expect all the Good and Evil of which his Life was capable: This Man, in his Temper uneasie, and piqu'd by a certain Partiality of *Cæsar*'s to his Disadvantage, could not satisfie a Sedate Bloody Humour by any less Reparation than his Ruin; and having[a] a revengeful Biass of Mind, a short Memory of Kindnesses, and an indelible Resentment of Wrongs, resolv'd to cancel an odious Benefit, by a pleasing Injury: To this Determination he was prompted by the worst *only Good* Quality a Man can have, an undaunted Courage, which fermented in Him a restless and *Gnawing* Meditation of his *Enemy's, that is, his Benefactor's Death*; A Thought befitting the Greatness of his Ambition, and the Largeness of his pernicious Capacity; His Capacity which consisted in a skilful Dissimulation of his Faults; for being full of those Vices which nearly approach, and easily assume the Resemblance of Virtue, and seldom throw a Man into visible and obvious Follies, he so well accommodated his ill Qualities to the good ones of those with whom he Convers'd, that he was very well with the best Men by a Similitude of their Manners; His Avarice obtain'd the Frugal; his Spleen, and Disrelish of Joy, the Sober and Abstinent; His Envy, and Hatred of Superiors, the Asserters of Publick Liberty: This considerable Wretch skilfully warm'd and urg'd some of his own Temper, whom he knew ready for any great Mischief, to pull down the Overgrown *Cæsar*, and ensnar'd others by the specious Pretence of a sincere Love to his Country, to meet all Hazards for her Recovery; These illustrious Ruffians, who

---

[a] having] having through *o1*

The Christian Hero

were indeed Men of the most Weight, and the boldest Spirits of the *Roman* Empire, design'd to dispatch him in the Eye of all the World, in open Senate; but neither their Quality or Accomplishments were great enough to support 'em in so Nefarious an Attempt, without there could be an Expedient thought of, to give it a more sacred Esteem, than any of their Characters could inspire: 'Twas therefore necessary to make *Marcus Brutus* of the Conspiracy.

This Gentleman possess'd the very Bosom of *Cæsar*, who having had a Notorious Intrigue with his Mother, was believ'd to have thought him his Son; but whether that, or an Admiration of his Virtue, was the cause of his Fondness, He had so tender a regard for him, that at the Battel of *Pharsalia* he gave it in Orders to the whole Army, if he would not take Quarter to let him escape: He was, like *Cæsar*, addicted to Letters and Arms, and tho' not equal to him in his *Capacity for either*, above him in the use of both. He never drew his Sword but with a design to serve his Country, nor ever Read with any other purpose but to subdue his Passions, so that he had from Books rather an habit of Life than a faculty of Speech; in his Thoughts as well as Actions he was a strict Follower of Honesty and Justice; all he said, as well as all he did, seem'd to flow from a publick and unbiass'd Spirit: He had no occasion for the Powers of Eloquence to be able to persuade, for all Men knew 'twas their Interest to be of his Mind; and he had before he spoke that first Point, the[a] good will of his Audience, for every Man's Love of himself

[a] the] of the *o1*

[15] made him a Lover of *Brutus*. He | had this Eminence without the least taint of Vanity, and a great Fame seem'd not so much the Pursuit, as the Consequence of his Actions: Thus should he do a thing which might be liable to Exception, Men would be more apt to suspect their own Judgment than his Integrity, and believe whatever was the Cause of the Action, it must be a good one since it mov'd him: And tho' a perfect Love of Mankind was the Spring of all he acted, that Human Temper never threw him into Facility, but since he knew an ungrounded Compassion to one Man might be a Cruelty to another, mere Distresses without Justice to plead for 'em could never prevail upon him, but, all Gentle as he was, he was impregnable to the most repeated Importunity, even that of his own good Nature.

Such was the Renown'd *Brutus*, and one would think a Man who had no ill Ambition to satisfie, no loose Passions to indulge, but whose Life was a Regular, Easie, and Sedate Motion, should be in little Temptation of falling into a Plot; but ill Men, where they cannot meet a convenient Vice, can make use of a Virtue to a base purpose.

He was Lineally Descended from the famous *Brutus*, that extinguish'd the *Tarquins*, whose Debauches and Cruelties made a Regal Name in *Rome* [16] as justly odious, as | that of the *Bruti* venerable for the Extirpation of it;[a] and *Cæsar* had very lately, in the midst of an absolute and unlimited Power, betray'd a Fantastick Ambition of being call'd King, which render'd him Obnoxious to the Malice of the Conspirators and the Virtue of *Brutus*. This was the

[a] for the Extirpation of it;] for it's extirpation, *o1*[1]

The Christian Hero

Place where the Magnanimity of that Patriot seem'd most accessible, for 'twas obvious, that He who wanted nothing else to spur him to Glorious Attempts, must be also Animated by the Memory of Illustrious Ancestors, and not like narrow and degenerate Spirits, be satisfied with the Fantask of Honour deriv'd from others, from whom, without a Similitude of Virtue, 'tis an unhappy distinction to descend.

Yet however hopeful this Handle appear'd, they could not so abruptly attempt upon his awful Character, as immediately to propose the Murder to him, without some distant Preparation of Mind to receive it. There were therefore these Words frequently dropt in his way, from unknown Hands: Thou art no longer *Brutus*; Thou art asleep, *Brutus*; and the like; by which Artifice he grew very Thoughtful and busie with himself, about the purpose of these Advertisements; One of such Moments *Cassius* took hold of, and opened to him the great Design for the Liberty of his Country from | *Cæsar*'s Usurpation: There needed no more to make him do a thing, but his Belief that 'twas Just; He soon consented that[a] *Cæsar* deserv'd to Die, and since he did, to Die by his Hand: Gaining this Personage, made all ripe for Execution, and *Cassius* possess'd a full Satisfaction, in that he had engag'd a Man in the Attempt, who in the Eyes of the People, instead of being sully'd by it, would stamp a Justice and Authority upon the Action; whose confirm'd Reputation was sufficient to expiate a Murder, and consecrate an Assassination.

Yet tho' his Justice made him readily consent to

[a] that *add. 10*

Cæsar's Death, his Gratitude upon Reflection shook his Resolution to Act in it; all which Conflict with himself we cannot view without the Incident of *Porcia*'s Story.

This Lady observ'd her Husband fall on a sudden from an easie, placid and fond, into a troubled, short and distracted Behaviour; she saw his Mind too much employ'd for the conjugal Endearments, and kind Tendernesses, in which she was usually happy, yet upon this Observation grew neither Jealous or Sullen, but mourn'd his Silence of his Affliction to her with as deep a Silence: This Lady, I say, this noble *Roman* Wife turn'd all her Suspicion upon her self, and modestly believ'd 'twas^a her Incapa|city for bearing so great a Secret, as that which discompos'd the stedfast *Brutus*, made him conceal from her an Affliction, which she thought she had a Title to participate; and therefore resolv'd to know of her self, whether his Secrecy was a Wrong to her before she would think it so; to make this Experiment, she gave her self a deep Stab in the Thigh, and thought if she could bear that Torture, she could also that of a Secret; the Anguish and Concealment of her Wound threw her into a Fever, in that condition she thus spoke to her Husband.

Vid. Mr. Duke's Translation of the Life of Brutus.

"I, *Brutus*, being the Daughter of *Cato*, was given "to you in Marriage, not like a Concubine, to par-"take only of the common Civilities of Bed and "Board, but to bear a Part in all your good and all "your evil Fortunes; and for my part, when I look "on you, I find no Reason to repent this Match; But "from Me, what Evidence of my Love, what Satis-

^a believ'd 'twas] believ'd that 'twas *o1*¹, *o1*²

"faction can you receive, if I may not share with you
"in your most hidden Griefs, nor be admitted to any
"of your Counsels, that require Secrecy and Trust;
"I know very well, that Women seem to be of too
"weak a Nature to be trusted with Secrets, but cer-
"tainly, *Brutus*, a Virtuous Birth and Education, and
"a Conversation with the Good and Honourable, are
"of some force | to the forming our Manners and [19]
"strengthning our Natural Weakness; and I can
"boast that I am the Daughter of *Cato*, and the Wife
"of *Brutus*. In which two great Titles, tho' before
"I put too little Confidence, yet now I have try'd
"my self, I find that even against Grief and Pain
"I am Invincible.

She then told him what she had done, but it is[a]
not easie to represent the kind Admiration such a
Discourse must give a[b] Husband, and the sweet
Transport that was drawn from their mutual Afflic-
tion, is too delicate a touch of Mind to be understood
but by a *Brutus* and a *Porcia*. Yet tho' he was not
too Wise to be tender to his Wife, when he had
unbosom'd himself, in spite of this last Action, and
a thousand nameless things, that occur'd to his
Memory to soften him, he left his Illustrious Heroin
in her Pains and her Sorrows, to pursue his publick
Resolutions. But he is gone, and she can burst into
those Tears which the Awe of his Virtue had made
her smother; for how alas shall the Heart of Woman
receive so harsh a Virtue, as to gratifie her Husband's
Will, by consenting to his Ruin? How shall she
struggle with her own Weakness and his Honour?
But while she lay in his Bosom she learn'd all the

[a] it is] 'tis *o1*¹   it 'tis *o1*²   [b] an *o1*¹, *o1*²

Gallantry of it, and when she ponders his Immortal
[20] Fame, | his Generous Justice, and *Roman* Resolution, her Mind enlarges into a Greatness, which surmounts her Sex, and her Affection: When she views him in the conspicuous part of Life, she can bear, nay Triumph in his Loss; but when she reflects and remembers their Tenderer Hours, thus would he Look, thus would he Talk, such was his Gesture, Mein, the Mirth, the Gaiety of the Man she Lov'd (which Instances are more intimate Objects of Affection, than Mens greater Qualities) then she is all Woman, she resigns the great but laments the agreeable Man; Can then my *Brutus* leave me? Can he leave these longing Arms for Fame? She has no just Notion of any higher Being to support her wretched Condition, but however her Female Infirmity made her languish, she has still Constancy enough to keep a Secret that concerns her Husband's Reputation, tho' she melts away in Tears, and pines into Death in Contemplation of her Sufferings.

Such must have been the Soliloquy of this Memorable Wife, who has left behind her an everlasting Argument, how far a Generous Treatment can make that tender Sex go even beyond the Resolution of Man, when we allow that they are by Nature form'd to Pity, Love and Fear, and we with an Impulse to Ambition, Danger and Adventure. |

[21] The World bore a Gloom and heavy Presage of *Cæsar*'s approaching Fate. 'Tis said Wild Beasts came into the most frequented Parts of the City, Apparitions in the Streets, unusual Illuminations in the Skies, and inauspicious Sacrifices damp'd the Hearts of all Men, but the Assassins, who with an

The Christian Hero

incredible Calm of Mind expected the opportunity of Satiating their Vengeance in the Blood of the Usurper; yet was not *Cassius* himself wholly unconcern'd, for tho' he was as great an Atheist as any among Us can pretend to be, he had the Weakness and Superstition at that time, to invoke a Statue of *Pompey* for his Assistance. It is as[a] observable, that *Cæsar*, the Evening before his Fate, in a Supper-conversation (at one of his Murderers Houses) on the subject of Death, pronounc'd a sudden one to be the most desireable, and a little shogg'd with reiterated ill Omens, and touch'd with the foreboding Dreams and Frights of a tender Wife, resolv'd to forbear going to the Senate on the Morning appointed for his *Execution*; which Difficulty *D. Brutus* undertook to get over; a Gentleman so superlatively excellent that way, that he could not only upon such an occasion appear Compos'd, but also in very good Humour; this *sneering* Ruffian rallied away his Fears, and with a very good Mein conducted his Friend to his Murder. |

When he came into the Senate, they rose to him, and with a pretended joint Petition for a Banish'd Man, the Assassins press'd about him, as soon as he was Seated: He severally check'd their Importunity, but while they were thus imploy'd, one of 'em gave the Sign by throwing his Robe over his Neck, another oppress'd with the Grandeur of the Attempt, made at him an irresolute Pass: He briskly oppos'd the Villain, and call'd him so; They all rush'd on him with drawn Ponyards, still he resisted 'till he saw *Brutus* coming on, then with a generous and disdainful

[a] as *add. 012*

Resignation, yielded to the stroke of a Pardon'd, Oblig'd and Rewarded Friend. But there are in *England* a Race of Men, who have this Action in the most profess'd Veneration, and who speciously miscall the Rancour, Malice and Hatred of all Happier and Higher than themselves, (which they have in common with *Cassius*) Gallantry of Mind, Disdain of Servitude, and Passion for publick Good, which they pretend to with *Brutus*; and[a] thus qualified with Ill, set up for Faction, Business, and Enmity to Kings. But 'tis to be hop'd these Men only run round 'till they're giddy, and when all things turn too, fancy themselves Authors of the Motion about 'em, and so take their Vertigo for their Force; for sure they have a futile Pretence to a good publick Spirit, who have an ill private one. |

[23] But there lies the Mighty *Cæsar*, an Eternal Instance how much too Generous and too Believing those unhappy Princes are, who depend upon the tie of Mens Obligations[b] to 'em, without having their Opinions on their side; for nothing hinders a Man's walking by the Principles of his Soul, but an Opportunity to exert 'em; when that occurs, the secret Enemy throws off his Mask and draws his Dagger.

Yet Reflections of this nature are somewhat foreign to our Purpose, we must therefore follow these bloody Men, to a Fate as violent as they gave their Benefactor; for 'twas in Providence to frustrate their Counsels, by turning that Virtue to their Ruin, which they had ensnared for their Protection. The fearless *Brutus* had too much Clemency, to make this Blow safe by the Execution of the nearest Adherents

---

[a] and *add.* *10* [b] *Misprinted* Obligtioans *10*

The Christian Hero

to *Cæsar*; His Safety consisted in his unbiass'd Mind and undaunted Resolution, which would not let him stoop to the taking away[a] any Life, below that of the greatest of Mankind.

However this Injury was repair'd to *Cæsar*, for he was voted a God in the very Place where he ceas'd to be a Man, which had been a good saving Clause, cou'd they have persuaded his Successor *Octavius* also, to have been contented with *Omnipotence*; but the young *Scholar* was so much enamour'd with | this [24] World, that he left his *Book* to disturb and rule it; and to compass his End, took upon him the hopeful Resolution of sparing no Man, from a Reflection perhaps that his Uncle was Ruin'd by Mercy in his Victories.

But it is[b] not our Business, to fall into an Historical Account of the various Occurrences, which happen'd in the War between the *Cæsarian* Army and that of the Conspirators, any farther than it is necessary[c] for judging how far the Principles they walk'd by were useful to 'em in their greatest Extremities: As *Brutus* one Evening sate Pensive and Revolving, the Passages of Life, and the Memory of *Cæsar*, occurr'd to him, now perhaps not as a Traitor, a Tyrant, or Usurper, but as one he Lov'd, and Murder'd; an Apparition appear'd (or he thought appear'd to him) which told him he was his Evil Genius and would meet him at *Philippi*, to which he calmly answer'd, *I'll meet thee there*: But he communicated a sad Impression which[d] this made upon him to *Cassius*, who

---

[a] to the taking away] to taking *01*[1]   [b] it is] 'tis *01*[1]   it 'tis *01*[2]
[c] any farther than it is necessary] but as it is necessary *01*[1], *01*[2]
[d] which *add. 10*

in an *Epicurean* manner gave him a Superficial Comfort, by Discourses of the Illusions, our Fancies our Dreams and our Sorrows Imprint upon the Mind, and make an imaginary a real Torment. Yet the Night before the Fatal Battel, he enquir'd (in case of a Defeat) his Resolution as to Flight and Death. To which *Brutus*: |

[25]
Vid. Mr. Duke's Translation of the Life of Brutus. Plut.

"When I was Young, *Cassius*, and unskilful in "Affairs, I was Engag'd I know not how into an "Opinion of Philosophy, which made me accuse *Cato* "for killing himself, as thinking it an Irreligious Act "against the Gods, nor any way[a] Valiant amongst "Men, not to submit to Divine Providence, nor be "able fearlessly to receive and undergo whatever shall "happen; but to fly from it: But now in the midst of "Dangers I am quite of another Mind, for if Pro"vidence shall not dispose what I now Undertake "according to our Wishes, I resolve to try no farther "Hopes, nor make any more Preparations for War, "but will Die contented with my Fortune, for I "already have given up my Life to the Service of "my Country on the *Ides* of *March*, and all the time "that I Lived since, has been with Liberty and "Honour.

However Gallant this Speech may seem at first Sight, it is upon Reflection a very mean one; for he urges no manner of Reason for his Desertion of the noble Principle of Resignation to the Divine Will, but his Dangers and Distresses; which indeed is no more than if he had plainly Confess'd, that all the Schemes we can form to our selves in a Compos'd and Prosperous Condition, when we come to be

[a] way *01*[1], *01*[2] *Misprinted* ways *10*

The Christian Hero

oppress'd with Calamities, vanish from us, and are but the Effects of luxu|riant Ease and good Humour, [26] and[a] languish and die away with 'em: But to make this a fair deduction from his Discourse,[b] let us Impartially (but with Tenderness and Pity) look at him in his last Pangs: At the Battel of *Philippi*, *Brutus* Commanded the Right, *Cassius* the Left of the Line: The first broke the opposite Wing of the Enemy, the second was himself forc'd. But by a Failure in their Orders and Intelligence, each was Ignorant of the other's Fortune; *Brutus* follow'd his Blow, and his Heat drove him too far before he thought of *Cassius*, whom at last, with a strong Detachment, he returns to Relieve. His Friend Retreated[c] to a rising Ground, to View and Bewail the Fate of their Cause, and Commanded an Officer to observe that Body marching towards him: The Gentleman soon found 'em Friends, and confidently Rid in amongst 'em; they as kindly enclos'd him to enquire News: Upon seeing this, the miserable *Cassius* concluded him taken by the Enemy, and giving all for lost, retir'd into a Tent, where he was by his own order Kill'd by a Servant.

Here *Brutus*, whom neither the Fondness of an excellent Wife, Obligations to a generous Friend, or a Message from the Dead cou'd Divert from meeting all Encounters, sinks and falls into the most extream Despair.|

He, with some others that escap'd the Pursuit, [27] retir'd to a Thicket of a Wood, where also finding they were trac'd, 'twas propos'd still to Fly: But he,

[a] which *o1*[1], *o1*[2]   [b] *Misprinted* Discouse, *10*
[c] Retreated] had Retreated *o1*[1], *o1*[2]

after having express'd[a] a Satisfaction (but a false one, since he could not live with it) in his Integrity, which he preferr'd to the Successes of his Enemies, ran upon his Sword, and transfix'd that great Heart with a superfluous Blow, which sure was before Stabb'd with the killing Reflection upon *Et tu Brute?*

Here let us throw a Veil over this mistaken Great Man, and if possible cover him from Human Sight for ever, that his seduc'd and *Ambiguous* Virtue may be no more Prophan'd, as an Umbrage to the Counsels of Perjur'd Friends, Sacrilegious Regicides, and implacable Desperadoes.

Now the use we make of these Reflections, is, that since we have seen the mighty *Cæsar* himself fall into Superstition at the Thought of his Exit, since *Cato*'s firm Constancy, *Brutus* his[b] generous Zeal, and *Cassius* his[c] steady Malice, all ended in the same Dereliction of themselves, and Despondence at last, we may justly conclude, that whatever Law we may make to ourselves, from the Greatness of Nature or the Principles of Philosophy[d] for the Conduct and Regulation of Life, is it self but an Artificial Passion, by which we vainly hope to subdue those that are Natural, and | which will certainly rise or fall with our Disappointment or Success, and we that are liable to both are highly concern'd to be prepar'd for either: At which Perfection there is no nearer way to arrive, but by attending our own Make, and observing by what means human Life, from its simple and rural Happiness, swell'd into the weighty Cares and Dis-

[a] after having express'd] after he had expressed *o1¹, o1²*
[b] Brutus his] Brutus's *o1¹, o1²*   [c] Cassius his] Cassius's *o1¹, o1²*
[d] from the Greatness of Nature or the Principles of Philosophy, *add. o1²* Philosophy *10*

tractions with which it is at present Enchanted; and from this Knowledge of our Misery, *Extract* our Satisfaction.

CHAP. II

MAN is a Creature of so mix'd a Composure, and of a[a] Frame so Inconsistent and Different from *Its* self, that it easily speaks his Affinity to the highest and meanest Beings; that is to say, he is made of Body and Soul, he is at once an *Engine*[b] and an *Engineer*: Tho' indeed both that Body and Soul[c] act in many Instances separate and independent of each other: For when he Thinks, Reasons and Concludes, he has not in all that Work the least Assistance from his Body: His finest Fibres, purest Blood, and highest Spirits are as brute and distant from a Capacity of Thinking as his very Bones; and the Body is so mere a Machine, that it Hungers, | Thirsts, [29] Tastes[d] and Digests, without any exerted Thought of the Mind to command that Operation: Which when he observes upon himself, he may, without deriving it from Vapour, Fume or Distemper, believe that his Soul may as well Exist out of, as in that Body from which it borrows nothing to make it capable of performing its most perfect Functions. This may give him hopes, that tho' his Trunk return to its native Dust he may not all Perish, but the Inhabitant of it may remove to another Mansion; especially since he knows only Mechanically that

[a] of a *add. 10*
[b] Misprinted *Engin 10*
[c] Soul] Soul too *01¹, 01²*
[d] *Misprinted* Tasts *10*

they have, not Demonstratively how they have, ev'n a present Union.

And since this Mind has a Consciousness and superior Reflection upon its own Being and Actions, and that Thoughts flow in upon it, from it knows not what Source, it is not Unnatural for it to conceive, that there is something of a Nature like it self, which may, Imperceptibly,[a] act upon it, and where it cannot deduce its reasonable Performances from any corporeal Beginning, draw Hopes or Fears from some Being thus capable to Impress Pleasure or Torment; which Being it cannot but suppose its Author.

But this its Author is Incomprehensible to the Soul (which he has thought fit to Imprison in Sense and Matter) but as he is pleas'd to reveal himself, and bestow upon it an Expectation of its Enlargement; yet were we to take the Account which Poetical Writers give, and suppose a Creature with these Endowments wandring among other wild Animals, the Intelligent[b] Savage would not be contented with what Rapine or Craft could gain from his Brethren Beasts, but his Condition would still be as necessitous for his better Part; and his dark natural Enquiry would make him, for want of a more just Knowledge of his Creator, fall into Superstition, and believe every Fountain, Grove and Forest inhabited by some peculiar Deity, that bestow'd upon Mankind the Stream, the Shade and the Breeze.

But we are inform'd that the[c] wonderful Creator of all Things, after he had given the Rivers to Flow, the Earth to bring Forth, and the Beasts to Feed,

---

[a] Imperceptibly,] Imperceptibly to it, $o1^1$, $o1^2$ [b] Intelligible $o1^1$
[c] a $o1^1$, $o1^2$

The Christian Hero

saw and approv'd his Work, but thought a dumb Brute and Mechanick World an imperfect Creation 'till inhabited by a conscious[a] Being, whose Happiness should consist in Obedience to, and a Contemplation on him and his *Wonders*.

For this Reason Man was created with intellectual Powers and higher Faculties, who immediately beheld with Joy and Rapture, a World made for the Support and Admiration of his new Being; how came he into this happy happy State! whence the Order! the Beauty! the *Melody* of this *Living* Gar|den! Are [31] the Trees Verdant? Do the Birds Sing? Do the Fountains Flow for no other reason but to Delight and Entertain him? How does he pass through the most bright and delicious Objects, and how does he *Burn* to utter himself upon the *Extatick* Motions which they give him! In such sweet Inquietude were the first Hours of the World spent, and in this Lassitude of Bliss and Thought our Parent fell into a profound Sleep, when his Maker, who knew how Irksome a lonely Happiness was to a sociable Nature, form'd out of his Side a Companion, Woman: He awak'd, and by a secret Simpathy beheld his Wife: He beheld his own rougher Make soften'd into Sweetness, and temper'd into Smiles: He saw a Creature (who[b] had as 'twere Heav'ns second Thought in her Formation) to whom[c] he cou'd communicate his Conceptions,[d] on whom[e] he could *Glut* his Eyes, with whom[f] he could Ravish his Heart: Over this Consort his Strength and Wisdom claim'd,

[a] nobler *o1¹* [b] which *o1¹, o1²* [c] which *o1¹, o1²*
[d] Thoughts, *o1¹, o1²* [e] which *o1¹, o1²*
[f] with whom] on which *o1¹, o1²*

but his Affection resign'd, the Superiority: These both *Equal* and both *Superior* were to live in a perfect Tranquility, and produce as happy a Progeny: The Earth and all its Fruit were theirs, Except only one Tree: Which light *Injunction* was all that was requir'd of 'em as an Instance of their Obedience and Gratitude to his Bounty, who had giv'n 'em everything else. But such was their Vanity and Ingratitude, that they soon forgot the Dependance suitable to a borrow'd Being, and were deluded into an empty hope of becoming by their Transgression like their Creator, and (tho' just Born of the Dust) proud enough from that No-Existence to disdain one that was Precarious: They did[a] *therefore Eat* and were Undone; they offended God, and like all *their* succeeding Criminals against him, were conscious that they did so. Innocence and Simplicity were banish'd their Bosoms, to give way to Remorse and Conviction. Guilt and Shame are the new Ideas they have pluck'd from the Tree of Knowledge: Their affronted Creator pronounces upon 'em a Sentence which they now think more supportable than the Pain of his offended Presence, which he withdrew; and commanded Nature to give 'em no further voluntary Obedience; so that he was now to extort from her the continuance of their wretched Condition by Toil and Labour, and she to bring forth Heirs to it with Pangs and Torture.

This is the Account we have from a certain neglected Book, which is call'd, and for its genuine Excellence above all other Books deservedly call'd THE SCRIPTURE: And methinks we may be

[a] did *add.* 10

The Christian Hero

convinc'd of the Truth of this History of our Parents, by the infallible Spots and Symptoms of their Here-|ditary Disease in our Tempers, Pride and Ingrati- [33] tude: For what is more natural to us, than by an unreasonable Self-opinion, (tho' we cannot but feel that we are but mere Creatures and not of our selves) to assume to our selves the Praise and Glory of our Capacities and Endowments! and how Lazy, how unwilling are we to *Eradicate* the deep and inward Satisfaction of Self-admiration? However, it must be confess'd, that 'tis the most senseless and stupid of all our Infirmities, for 'till you can remember and recount to us, when that Thinking, *Throbbing* Particle within, first resolv'd to *Wear* a Body, when it spun out its Arteries, Fibres and Veins, contriv'd the warm circulating Stream that runs through 'em, when you first ventur'd to let the Heart pant, the Lungs suck Air, and at last to lanch the whole tender Machine into the hazard of Motion; 'till, I say, you can acquaint us with all this, you must kneel and fall down before him, by whom you were thus Fearfully and Wonderfully Made.

But the first Pair, now suspicious of each other, banish'd the more immediate Influence and Presence of their Almighty Protector, were liable (Naked and Distress'd as they were) to be entangled by the Thorn and the Brier, and torn by the Lion and Wolf, who have ever since been prompted to fly in the | Faces [34] of the detested Ingrates: Therefore the increasing World, for their Defence against Themselves, and other Animals, were oblig'd to go into Contracts and Policies, so that human Life (by long Gradation) ascended into an Art: The Tongue was now to Utter one thing, and the Bosom to Conceal another; and from a desire of Superiority in our deprav'd Natures, was bred that unsatisfied *Hunger* Ambition; a monstrous Excrescence of the Mind, which makes Superfluity, Riches, Honour and Distinction, but mere Necessities of Life, as if 'twere our Fate in our fallen Condition (lest a Supply of what frugal Nature desires should be obtain'd) to find out an Indigence foreign to us, which is incapable of being reliev'd, and (which to confirm our Want and Misery) increases with its Acquisitions: Under this leading Crime, are Envy, Hatred, Cruelty, Cunning, Craft and Debate, Muster'd and Arm'd; and a Battalion of Diseases, Torments and Cares, the natural Effects of those Evils, become our bosom Companions; from which no Arms can rescue, no Flight secure us but a Return to that God, in whose Protection only is our Native lost Seat of Rest and Tranquility. To which Abode since our Expulsion we cannot dare to approach, but Guilt which runs even to Succours it [35] knows vain, makes us, with our first Parents | in the same Circumstances, hide from Omnipresence: I said in the same Circumstances, for we have not only implicitly committed their Crime, as we were in them, but do also actually repeat it in our own Persons: For when a Created Being relinquishes the Power of its Creator, and instead of relying on his Conduct and Government, draws to it self an independent Model of Life, what does it but pluck from the Tree of Knowledge, and attempt a Theft of Understanding, from him who is Wisdom it self? This is a tremendous Consideration, yet is there not that Man breathing, who has any where placed his

The Christian Hero

Confidence but in God, and considers seriously his own Heart, but feels its Weight, nor can the Bosom under it receive any Impression, but that of endless Despair.

But behold the Darkness disperses, and there is still Hope breaking in upon our Sorrow, by the Light of which we may again lift up our Eyes, and see our Maker: For in the midst of our deserv'd Misery, our Reconciliation is coming on through a Mediator, who[a] is perfectly unconcern'd in our Crime:[b] But tho' innocent of our Transgression, assumes that and our Nature, and, as an Atonement for us, offers his Life a Ransom, with this regard on our Part, that as it is an Expiation, it is also an Example: An Example to instruct us, that not only[c] the first Command laid upon us was a reasonable | one, but also the present Life easie and supportable, for he himself voluntarily undergoes it in its greatest Calamities: He who had all things in his Power, and wanted all things, by inforcing an abstinent use of Wealth, and patient enduring of Poverty, restores us not only to the Bliss of leading this Life with Satisfaction and Resignation to the Divine Will (which only is our true Life) but by a short Passage through a momentary Death, translates us to an happy everlasting Existence, incapable of Sorrow, Weariness or Change: To accomplish which great Revolution, our glorious Deliverer from our selves design'd to Establish his Empire, not by Conquest, but a Right much more lasting, *Arduous* and *Indisputable Conviction*; For our Slavery being Intellectual and in our own Bosoms,

---

[a] who] who as such *01¹*   [b] cause: *01¹*
[c] that not only] *Misprinted* that only *10*

the Redemption must be there also; Yet the World, Inchanted with its own imaginary Notions of Freedom, knew not how to receive so Abstracted a Manumission, but contemn'd the Promise of Restoration to *Life* and *Liberty*, from a poor Man who himself enjoy'd none of the Advantages which arise from those *Dear* (but *Misunderstood*) Appellations.

May we then without Blame approach and behold this Sacred and Miraculous Life? How, alas! shall we Trace the Mysterious Steps of God and Man? [37] How consider him | at once in Subjection to, and Dominion over Nature?

The most Apposite, (tho' most slow) Method of reducing the World to its Obedience, was that our Blessed Saviour should appear in the despicable Attire which he did, without any of those attendant Accidents which attract the Eye, and charm the Imagination: For the Knowledge which he was to Introduce, being an Eternal Truth; the proper Mansion for it was in the Reason and Judgment, into which when it had once enter'd, it was not to be remov'd by any Impressions upon the lower Faculties, to which it was not to be[a] beholden for a Reception. There is not therefore one Instance in the New Testament of Power exerted to the Destruction, tho' so many to the Preservation of Mankind: But to a degenerate Race, he that Heals, is less valu'd than he that Kills: Confusion, Terror, Noise and Amazement, are what only strike servile Minds; but Order, Symmetry, silent Awe, Blessings and Peace are Allurements to the Open, Simple, Innocent and Truly knowing; yet the very Nation among whom

[a] to be *add. 10*

The Christian Hero

the Holy *Jesus* Descended to Converse, had (if we may so speak) in a manner[a] tir'd Heav'n with appearing in the more Pompous Demonstrations of its Power: They pass'd through Waves *Divided* and *Erect* for their March, they were supernaturally Fed in a Wilderness, a Mountain shook, and Thunder utter'd their Law; Nations were Destroy'd to gain them Inheritance! But they soon forgot these Benefits, and upon the least Cessation of Fear and Miracle, they deserted their Creator, and return'd to their own Handywork Deities, who were as senseless of their Makers, as themselves were of theirs.

Thus short-liv'd is Wonder, and thus Impotent to fix (what we have said our Law-giver design'd) Conviction. For which Reason our Astonishment in the New Testament is more sparingly rais'd, and that only to awaken our Attention to Plain, Easie, and Obvious Truths (which support themselves when receiv'd) by the Authority of Miracle.

We Read that he was led into a Wilderness, where *Matt.* 4. he wonderfully bore Hunger and Want for Forty Days; in the height of which Exigence and Necessity, the Tempter came to him and Urg'd him, if he were the Son of God, to Relieve his present Misery, by turning the Stones[b] into Bread; which Attempt when he found Fruitless, and observ'd that he wou'd Use no supernatural Relief, but bear Human Nature and its Infirmities, he Attacks him[c] the most acceptable way to our *Weakness* in the Supplies of Pride and Vanity: He showed him the Kingdoms and Glory of the World, (which he had Purchased from Man by

---

[a] in a manner *add*. *01*²   [b] Stones] Stones near him *01*¹, *01*²
[c] him] him in *01*¹, *01*²

[39] his Defection from | God) and offer'd him the Dominion of 'em if he would Worship him; but our Lord Contemn'd this also, and in his Want and Poverty retir'd into a private Village; where and in the Adjacent Parts if the Necessitous Man lay in Obscurity, the merciful God did not, for he never discontinued his Visible benign Assistance, to the Relief of the Diseas'd, the Possess'd and the Tormented.

Matt. 5. In his admirable Sermon upon the Mount, he gives his Divine Precepts in so easie and familiar a manner, and which[a] are so well adapted to all the Rules of Life and right Reason, that they must needs carry throughout a self evident Authority to all that Read 'em; to those that Obey 'em, from the firm Satisfaction which they Inspire; to those that neglect 'em, from the Anxiety that naturally attends a contrary Practice: There is the whole Heart of Man discover'd by him that Made it, and all our secret Impulses to Ill, and false appearances of Good, expos'd and detected: Among other excellent Doctrines, one which methinks must be, to those who are so harden'd as to read the Divine Oracles with Unbelief, an irrefragable Argument of his Divinity:

Matt. 6. 6. *But when thou Prayest, enter into thy Closet, and when thou hast shut thy Door, Pray to thy Father which is in Secret, and thy Father which seeth in Secret, shall* [40] *reward thee Openly.* Now it cannot enter in | to the Heart of Man, that any but God could be the Author of a Command so abstracted from all worldly Interests; for how absurd were it in a Being, that had not an intercourse with our Souls, or knew not their most secret Motions, to direct our Application to it

[a] and which] and those themselves *o1*[1]   and those *o1*[2]

The Christian Hero

self,[a] so strictly apart,[b] and out of the Observation of any Power less than Ubiquitary?

There came to him a Captain, in the behalf of his Servant, grievously tormented with a Palsie: Our Lord promis'd him to come and heal him, but the Soldier (with an openness and sincerity of Mind peculiar to his Profession) who[c] could not believe in, or serve him, but with his whole Heart, told him, he knew Nature was[d] in his Power with as despotick a Subjection, as his Men were under his, begg'd him only to speak him whole, and he knew he would be so: Our Saviour extoll'd his honest, frank and unreserved Confidence, gave him a suitable Success, sending him away with this Glorious Eulogium, that he had not found such Faith, no not in *Israel*! *Matt.* 8.

Thus did he bestow Mercy and Salvation upon the easie and common terms of ordinary *Friendship*, as if there needed nothing to make him, but believing he would be, their Benefactor. And, who in the least Affairs, is a Friend to him that distrusts him? |

In plain and apt Parable, Similitude and Allegory, he proceeded daily to inspire and enforce the Doctrine of our Salvation; but they of his Acquaintance, instead of receiving what they could not oppose, were offended at the Presumption, of being wiser than they: Is not this the Carpenter's Son, is not his Mother call'd *Mary*, his Brethren, *James*, *Joseph*, *Simon* and *Judas*? They could not raise their little Ideas above the consideration of him, in those Circumstances familiar to 'em, or conceive that he who appear'd not more Terrible or Pompous, should have [41] *Matt.* 13. 55.

---

[a] self *add.* 10   [b] so strictly apart,] to be so strictly apart, *o1¹, o1²*
[c] who *add. o1²*   [d] was *add. o1²*

any thing more Exalted than themselves; he in that Place[a] therefore would not longer[b] ineffectually exert a Power which was incapable of Conquering the Prepossession of their narrow and mean Conceptions.

Matt. 15.   Multitudes follow'd him, and brought him the Dumb, the Blind, the Sick and Maim'd; whom when their Creator had Touch'd, with a second Life they Saw, Spoke, Leap'd and Ran; in Affection to him, and Admiration of his Actions, the Crowd could not leave him, but waited near him Three Days, 'till they were almost as faint and helpless as others they brought for Succour: He had compassion on 'em, commanded 'em to be seated, and with Seven Loaves, and a few little Fishes, Fed four thousand Men, besides Women and Children: Oh the Extatick Enter|tainment, when they could behold their Food immediately increase, to the Distributer's Hand, and see their God in Person, Feeding and Refreshing his Creatures: Oh Envied Happiness! But why do I say Envied, as if our Good God did not still preside over our temperate Meals, chearful Hours, and innocent Conversations.

But tho' the sacred Story is every where full of Miracles, not inferior to this, and tho' in the midst of those Acts of Divinity, he never gave the least hint of a Design to become a Secular Prince, or in a Forcible or Miraculous manner to cast off the *Roman* Yoke they were under, and restore again those disgrac'd Favourites of Heav'n, to its former Indulgence, yet had not hitherto the Apostles themselves (so *deep set* is our Natural Pride) any other than hopes of Worldly Power, Preferment, Riches and Pomp:

[a] in that Place *add.* 10   [b] longer] longer there $o1^1, o1^2$

The Christian Hero

For *Peter*, who it seems ever since he left his Net and his Skiff, Dreamt of nothing but being a great Man, was utterly undone to hear our Saviour explain to 'em, upon an Accident of Ambition among 'em, that his Kingdom was not of this World; and was so scandaliz'd, that he, whom he had so long follow'd, should suffer the Ignominy, Shame and Death which he foretold, that he took him aside and said, *Be it far from thee, Lord, this shall not be unto thee:* For which he suffer'd a severe Reprehen|sion from his Master, having[a] in his View the Glory of Man, rather than that of God. *Matt.* 1. 22.[1] [43]

The great Change of things began to draw near, when the Lord of Nature thought fit as a Saviour and Deliverer to make his publick Entry into *Jerusalem*, with more than the Power and Joy, but none of the Ostentation and Pomp of a Triumph: He came Humble, Meek and Lowly; with an unfelt new Extasie, Multitudes strow'd his way with Garments and Olive-branches, Crying with loud Gladness and Acclamation, *Hosannah to the Son of* David, *Blessed is he that cometh in the Name of the Lord!* At this Great King's Accession to his Throne, Men were not Ennobled but Sav'd; Crimes were not Remitted, but Sins Forgiven; he did not bestow Medals, Honours, Favours, but Health, Joy, Sight, Speech! The first Object the Blind ever saw, was the Author of Sight, while the Lame Ran before, and the Dumb repeated the *Hosannah!* Thus Attended, he Entred into his own House, the Sacred Temple, and by his Divine *Matt.* 21.

[a] having] as having *o1*, *o2*

---

[1] The correct reference is Matthew 16. 22. The error was corrected in the fourth edition.

Authority Expell'd Traders and Worldlings that Prophan'd it; and thus did he, for a time, use a great and despotick Power, to let Unbelievers understand, that 'twas not want of, but Superiority to all Worldly Dominion, that made him not exert it: But is this then the Saviour, is this the Deliverer? shall this Obscure | *Nazerene* command *Israel*, and sit in the Throne of *David*? such[a] were the unpleasant Forms that ran in the Thoughts of the then Powerful in *Jerusalem*, upon the most Truly Glorious Entry that ever Prince made; for there was not one that follow'd him, who was not in his Interest; their Proud and Disdainful Hearts, which were petrified[b] with the Love and Pride of this World, were impregnable to the Reception of so mean a Benefactor, and were now enough exasperated with Benefits to Conspire his Death: Our Lord was sensible of their Design, and prepar'd his Disciples for it, by recounting to 'em now more distinctly what should befall him; but *Peter* with an ungrounded Resolution, and in a Flush of Temper, made a Sanguine Protestation; that tho' all Men were offended in him, yet would not he be offended. It was a great Article of our Saviour's Business in the World, to bring us to a Sense of our Inability, without God's Assistance, to do any thing Great or Good; he therefore told *Peter*, who thought so well of his Courage and Fidelity, that they would both fail him, and ev'n he should deny him Thrice that very Night.

But what Heart can conceive? What Tongue utter the Sequel? Who is that yonder Buffeted, Mock'd and Spurn'd? Whom do they Drag like a

---

[a] such *add. 10*   [b] *Misprinted* Putrified *10*

Felon? Whither do they | carry my Lord, my King, [45] my Saviour and my God? And will he Die to expiate those very Injuries? See where they have Nail'd the Lord and Giver of Life! How his Wounds blacken! His Body writhes, and Heart heaves with Pity, and with Agony! Oh Almighty Sufferer, look down, look down from thy Triumphant Infamy; Lo he inclines his Head to his Sacred Bosom! Hark he Groans, see he Expires! The Earth trembles, the Temple rends, the Rocks burst, the Dead Arise; Which are the Quick? Which are the Dead? Sure Nature, all Nature is departing with her Creator.

CHAP. III

THERE was nothing in our Saviour's own Deportment, or in the Principles He introduc'd for our Conduct, but what was so far from Opposing, that they might naturally fall in with the Statutes or Forms of any Civil Government whatever, and regarded 'em no otherwise than to make us more Obedient to 'em: Yet the Professors of this Doctrine were told they were to meet but very little Quarter, for the acceptable Service they were to do 'em, but must lay down their very Lives to bring Us to a Contempt of their | Grandeur in Comparison of Greater [46] and Higher Pursuits: In order to this Great End, their Despicable Artillery were Poverty and Meekness; the consideration therefore of those Arms is no Digression from our Purpose: It is in every Body's Observation with what disadvantage a Poor Man enters upon the most Ordinary Affairs, much more disputing with the whole World, and in[a] contradiction of the Rich, that is, the Wise; For as certainly as Wealth gives Acceptance and Grace to all that its Possessor says or does, so Poverty creates Disesteem, Scorn and Prejudice to all the Undertakings of the Indigent: The Necessitous Man has neither Hands, Lips, or Understanding, for his own, or Friends use, but is in the same condition with the Sick, with this Difference only, that his is an Infection no Man will Relieve, or Assist, or if he does, 'tis seldom with so much Pity, as Contempt, and rather for the Ostentation of the Physician, than Compassion on the Patient: It is a Circumstance, wherein a Man finds all the Good he deserves inaccessible, all the Ill unavoidable; and the Poor Hero is as certainly Ragged, as the Poor Villain Hang'd: Under these Pressures the Poor Man speaks with Hæsitation, undertakes with Irresolution, and acts with Disappointment: He is slighted in Mens Conversations, overlook'd in [47] their Assemblies, and beaten at | their Doors: But from whence alas has he this Treatment? from[b] a Creature that has only the Supply of, but[c] not an[d] Exemption from the Wants, for which he despises him: For such is the unaccountable Insolence of Man, that he will not see that he who is supported, is in the same Class of natural Necessity with him that wants a Support; and to be help'd, implies to be indigent. In a Word, after all you can say of a Man, conclude that he is Rich, and you have made him Friends; nor have you utterly overthrown a Man in the World's Opinion, 'till you have said he is

[a] in *add. 01²* [b] from *add. 01²* [c] but *add. 01²* [d] an *add. 01²*

The Christian Hero

Poor: This is the Emphatical Expression of Praise and Blame, for Men so stupidly forget their natural Impotence and Want, that Riches and Poverty have taken in our Imagination the place of Innocence and Guilt; he therefore that has suffer'd the Contumelies, Disappointments and Miseries which attend the Poor Man's Condition, and without running into base, indecent or servile Arts for his redress, hath[a] return'd upon an insolent World its Scorn. He (I say)[b] has fought a nobler Fight, Conquer'd greater Difficulties, and deserves a brighter Diadem, than ever Fortune bestow'd on the most fonded and most gaudy of her Favourites: But to capacitate ones self[c] for this hard Work, how necessary is that Sublime and Heroick Virtue, Meekness, a Virtue which seems the very | Characteristick of a Christian, and arises from a [48] great, not a groveling Idea of things: For as certainly as Pride proceeds from a mean and narrow view of the little Advantages about a Man's self, so Meekness is founded on the extended Contemplation of the Place we bear in the Universe, and a just Observation how little, how empty, how wavering are our deepest Resolves and Councils; and as (to a well taught Mind) when you've said an Haughty and Proud Man, you have spoke a narrow Conception, little Spirit, and despicable Carriage; so when you've said a Man's Meek and Humble, you've acquainted us, that such a Person[d] has arriv'd at the hardest Task in the World in an universal Observation round him, to be quick to see his own Faults and other Mens Virtues, and[e] at the height of pardoning every Man

---

[a] hath *add. 10* [b] (I say) *add. 10* [c] ones self *add. 10*
[d] that such a Person] that Person *01*¹ that that Person *01*² [e] and *add. 10*

sooner than himself; you've also[a] given us to understand, that to treat him kindly, sincerely and respectfully, is but a mere Justice to him that's ready to do us the same Offices: This Temper of Soul keeps us always awake to a just sense of things, teaches us that we are as well akin to Worms as to Angels, and as nothing is above these, so is nothing below those: It keeps our Understanding right[b] about us, so that all things appear to us great or little as they are in Nature, not as they are gilded or sullied by Accident and Fortune.

[49] Meekness is to the Mind, what a good Mein is to the Body, without which, the best Limb'd and finest Complection'd Person may be very Disagreeable; and with it, a very Homely and Plain one cannot be so; for a good Air supplies the Imperfection of Feature and Shape, by throwing a certain Beauty[c] on the whole, which covers[d] the disagreeableness[e] of the Parts; it has a State and Humility peculiar to its self above all Virtues, like the Holy Scripture, its sacred Record, where the highest things are express'd in the most easie Terms, and which carries throughout a condescending Explanation, and a certain Meekness of Stile.

With this Circumstance, and this ready Virtue, the faithful Followers of a Crucify'd Master were to shape their Course to an Eternal Kingdom, and with that in Prospect to contemn the hazards and disasters of a Cruel and Impenitent Generation. Great were the Actions and Sufferings of all our Blessed Saviour's

---

[a] you've also] and you've $o1^1$, $o1^2$
[b] Tight $o1^2$, $1o$
[c] a certain Beauty] an Harmony $o1^1$
[d] drowns $o1^1$
[e] Incapacities $o1^1$

The Christian Hero

Apostles, but St. *Paul* being peculiarly sent to Us who were or are Gentiles, he methinks more particularly challenges our regard: God who[a] bestow'd upon others supernaturally the Gift of Tongues, but not of Arts, thought therefore fit to make use of him already Master in some measure[b] of both, and qualified to converse with the politer World by his Acquaintance with their Studies, Laws and Customs: But tho' he shows himself by frequent brisk Sallies and quick Interrogatories, skilful in approaching the Passions by Rhetorick, yet he is very modest in any of those Ornaments, and strikes all along at the Reason, where he never fails to convince the attentive and unprejudic'd; and tho' his Person was very despicable (which to a Stranger is almost an insuperable[c] Inconvenience) yet such was the Power of the Commanding Truth which he utter'd, and his Skill how and when to utter it, that there every where appears in his Character, either the Man of Business, the Gentleman, the Hero, the Apostle, or the Martyr; which Eminence above the other Apostles, might well be expected from his Sanguine and Undertaking Complexion, temper'd by Education, and quickned by Grace: 'Tis true indeed, he had Oppos'd in the most Outragious and Violent manner this new Faith, and was accessary to[d] the Murder of the glorious Leader of the Army of Martyrs, St. *Stephen*; but that fierce Disposition fell off with the Scales from his Eyes, and God, who ever regards the Intention, chang'd his mistaken Method of serving him, and he is now ready to promote the same

[a] who *add. 01²*   [b] in some measure *add. 01²*
[c] Insupportable *01¹*   [d] in *01¹, 01²*

Religion by his Sufferings, which before he would have Extirpated by his Persecutions. He and his Companion had made very great | Progress in the Conversion both of Jews and Gentiles, but certain Unbelievers Prompted the Multitude to a Resolution at a general Assembly to Assassine 'em, but they advertis'd of it fled into *Lycaonia*, where their Actions and Eloquence were very Successful; but at *Lystra*, a certain poor Cripple (from his Mother's Womb) heard him with very particular Attention and Devotion, whom the Apostle (observing in his very Countenance his warm Contrition and Preparation of Soul to receive the Benefit) commanded to stand up, upon which he immediately Jump'd upon his Legs, and Walk'd: This Miracle alarm'd the whole City, who believ'd their Gods had descended in Human Shapes: *Barnabas* was immediately *Jove*, and *Paul* his *Mercury*: The Priest of *Jupiter* now is coming to Sacrifice to 'em with Oxen and Garlands; but they ran into the Multitude; we are Men like you, are subject to the same Weakness, Infirmities, and Passions with your selves: We, alas! are Impotent of the great things our selves have done; your and our Creator will no longer let you wander in the Maze and Error of your Vanities and false Notions of his Deity, but has sent us with Instances of his Omnipotence to awake you to a Worship worthy him, and worthy you. Oh graceful Passage to see the great Apostle oppose his own Success! Now| only his Vehemence, his Power and his Eloquence are too feeble when they are urgent against themselves; for with Prayers and Entreaties the Crowd could hardly be prevail'd upon, to forbear their Adoration. But this Applause,

The Christian Hero

like all other, was but a mere Gust, for the Malice of certain Jews follow'd 'em from *Iconium*, and quickly insinuated into the giddy Multitude, as much Rancour as they had before Devotion; who in a Tumultuary manner Ston'd St. *Paul*, and drag'd him as Dead,[a] out of the Gates of the City; but he bore their Affronts with much less Indignation than their Worship: Here was in a trice the highest and lowest condition, the most respectful and most insolent treatment that Man could receive; but Christianity, which kept his Eye upon the Cause not Effect of his Actions, (and always gives us a transient regard to transitory things,) depress'd him when Ador'd, exalted him when Affronted.

But these two excellent Men, tho' they had the Endearments of Fellow Suffering, and their Friendship heightned by the yet faster tie of Religion, could not longer accompany each other, but upon a Dispute about taking *Mark* with 'em, who it seems had before *Acts* 15. deserted 'em, their Dissention grew to the highest ver. 39. a Resentment between Generous Friends ever can, even[b] to part and estrange | 'em: But they did it [53] without Rancour, Malice, or perhaps Dis-esteem of each other; for God has made us, whether we observe it at the instant of being so or not, so much Instruments of his great and secret Purposes, that he has given every individual Man, I know not what peculiarly his own, which so much distinguishes him from all other Persons, that 'tis impossible, sometimes, for two of the same generous Resolutions, Honesty and Integrity to do well together; whether it be that Providence has so order'd it to distribute Virtue the

[a] drag'd him as Dead,] as Dead drag'd him *o1*¹, *o1*²   [b] even *add. 10*

56   *The Christian Hero*

more, or whatever it is, such is the frequent effect. For these noble Personages were forc'd to take different Ways, and in those were eminently useful in the same Cause; as you may have seen two Chymical Waters, asunder, shiningly transparent, thrown together, muddy and offensive.

Acts 11.[1] The Apostle was warn'd in a[a] Vision to go into *Macedonia*, whither he and his now Companion *Silas* accordingly went: At *Philippi* he commanded an Evil Spirit to depart out of a Young Woman; but her Master (to whom her distraction was a Revenue, which ceas'd by her future Inability to answer the Demands usually made to her,) with the ordinary method of hiding private Malice in publick Zeal, rais'd the Multitude upon 'em, as Disturbers of the [54] publick Peace, | and Innovators upon their Laws and Liberties: The Multitude hurry'd 'em to the Magistrates, who happening to be as wise as themselves, commanded 'em to be Stripp'd, Whipp'd, and clap'd in Gaol[b]: The Keeper receiving very strict orders for their safe Custody, put 'em in Irons in the Dungeon; the abus'd Innocents had now no way left for their redress, but applying to their God, who when all human Arts and Forces fail, is ready for our Relief, nor did St. *Paul* on less Occasions implore præternatural Assistance; *Nec Deus intersit nisi dignus vindice Nodus Inciderit*—

Horace's General Epistle to Piso's Verse 105.
    Let not a God approach the Scene,
    In cases for a God too[c] *mean.*

We must, to Men of Wit and Gallantry, quote

[a] a *add. 10*   [b] *Misprinted* Goal *10*   [c] to *or*1, *or*2

---

[1] The correct reference is Acts 16. The error was corrected in the fourth edition.

out of their own Scriptures. Their Generous way of Devotion, and begging Assistance, was giving Thanks for their present Extremities: In the midst of their Sores and Chains, they Sang Hymns and Praises to their Creator: Immediately the Bolts flew, the Manacles fell off, the Doors were opened, and the Earth shook: The Gaoler awakes in Terrour, and believing all under his Custody escap'd, went to dispatch himself; but St. *Paul* calls to him, he comes and beholds his Prisoners detain'd by nothing but[a] their amazing Liberty; the Horror, Sorrow, Torture, [55] and Despair of a Dungeon, turn'd into the Joy, the Rapture, the Hallelujah, the Extasie of an Heav'n; He fell Trembling at the Apostles Feet, resign'd himself to his Captives, and felt in himself the happy Exchange of his Liberty, for that Yoke in which alone is[b] perfect Freedom. Early the next Morning, upon this stupendious occasion, the Magistrates sent Orders those Men might be Releas'd: But St. *Paul*, who knew he had Law on his side, and that his being a Prisoner made him not the less[c] a Gentleman and a *Roman*, scorn'd their pretended Favour, nor would regard their Message, 'till they had themselves in as publick a manner acknowledg'd their Offence, as they had committed it, which they did by attending 'em in the Gaol, and desiring in a Ceremonious manner they would leave the[d] City; upon which the Apostle accepted his Inlargement, and when he had settled what *Acts* 16. Business he had in that Town, left it and its Rulers to forget that painful Truth, which they had neither Power to gainsay, nor Ingenuity to acknowledge.

[a] nothing but *add.* $o1^2$
[b] is] there is $o1^1$
[c] not the less] nevertheless $o1^1$, $o1^2$
[d] their $o1^1$, $o1^2$

His taking leave of the Chief of the *Ephesian* Churches, is hardly to be Read without Tears, where, when he had reminded 'em of his whole Blameless, Disinterested, Humble, and Laborious Carriage, he acquaints 'em with his Resolution of going to *Jeru-* [56] *salem* | and never to return thither; he knew not, he said, what would particularly befal him there, but that in general, Afflictions, Distresses and Indignities were the Portion of his Life, which he was ready to hazard or lay down in a Cause which has a certain sweetness in it, that can make a Man embrace his Chains, and enjoy his Miseries; what could be answer'd to his gallant Declaration and Behaviour but what they did, who *All wept sore, and fell on St. Paul's Neck, and Kissed him? Sorrowing most of all for the Words which he spake, that they should see his Face no more.* Certain Jews of *Asia* were glad to see him again at *Jerusalem*, and inflam'd the City with their Personal Knowledge of his Carriage, to the disparagement of the Temple, and the Rites of their Nation: Upon which he had been torn to Pieces, had he not been Rescu'd by the Commanding Military Officer there; of whom (going with him as a Prisoner into the Castle) he obtain'd the Liberty of speaking to the People: They heard him with great attention, 'till he contradicted their Monopoly of God; at which they lost all Order and Patience. But Opposition was so far from dispiriting, that it did but quicken his Resolution; for his great Heart, instead of Fainting and Subsiding, rose and biggen'd in proportion [57] to any growing Danger that[a] threatened him; | however he is carry'd to[b] his Imprisonment, but not ev'n

Acts 20. 38.

---

[a] that] he saw *o1*, *o2*   [b] into *o1*, *o2*

The Christian Hero

there to be without debate, for he is by the Commander's Order to be Scourg'd, to which he does[a] not Passively, or basely submit, but asserts his *Roman* Privilege, and Exemption from such Indignities.

He was thereupon next Morning brought down to a Trial by a Council of his own Nation, where upon his very opening his Mouth, the Chief Priest commanded him to be struck, for which he calls him Hypocrite and false Pretender to Justice, who could use a Man, he was to sit as Judge of, so Inhumanly; but his good Breeding being founded upon no less a Sanction than the Command of God, he immediately Recollects himself, and acknowledges his Error and Disrespect to the Dignity of his Office: Yet observing (by this treatment from the President of the Council) the usage he was to expect, by a very skilful turn he makes Friends in an Assembly unanimous in his Ruin, but in that only unanimous; for *Pharisees*, in which Sect he was Bred, composing part of the Court, he closes with their belief of a Resurrection, and there grounded the Cruelty he had met with among the Jews: This put 'em into so great a Flame, that to save him he was forcibly taken away into the place from whence he came: His[b] Enemies, gall'd to the quick at his | escape, Conspir'd to Kill [58] him, when (upon the High Priest's request) he should be remanded to a Trial: A Nephew of the Apostle's acquainted him with this; he was neither afraid or amaz'd at the Intelligence, but like a Man of Business and the World, discreetly and calmly order'd the Youth to be introduc'd to the Captain, whom he knew answerable for the Safety of his

Acts cap. 23.

---

[a] *Misprinted* do's *10*   [b] His] But his *o1¹, o1²*

Prisoner: The Officer in the Night sent him with a strong Party to *Fælix* the Governor of the Province, and directed his Accusers to follow him thither: Before *Fælix*, one *Tertullus*, a Mercenary Orator, baul'd an impertinent Harangue, introduc'd with false Praise of the Judge, and clos'd with false Accusation of the Prisoner, who with cogent plain Truths, and matter of Fact, baffled his barbarous Eloquence, and obtain'd so good a Sense of himself and his Innocence with the Viceroy, that he gave him a private Audience on the subject of his Faith; but instead of then making his Court to him, he fell upon his Excellency's own darling Vices, talk'd of Righteousness, Temperance, and Judgment,[a] with its Terrors for neglect of such Duties. In those Heathen times, it seems it was usual to have Excess, Wantonness, and Gluttony, to be[b] the Practice of Courts, and the Apostle so nearly touch'd his Lordship, that he fell into a sudden Dis|order before his Inferior, and dismiss'd him 'till another Season; he afterwards frequently was entertain'd by him, not without hopes of a Bribe, which was also, in very old Times, the way to the Favours of the Great.

But *Fælix* now leaving his Lieutenancy to *Festus*, this Friendless good Man was a proper Person for a Tool to his Vanity, by doing an obliging thing to the Jews, in leaving him still in Custody at his departure, and no less useful to his New Excellency to be Sacrific'd to 'em upon his Entry: For at their request to have him brought to *Jerusalem* (designing to dispatch him by the way) tho' he at first denied it, he afterwards propos'd it to the Apostle himself, to

---

[a] Abstinence *01*[1]   [b] to be *add. 01*[2]

The Christian Hero

have the Issue of his Tryal there: But he handsomly evaded his base Condescention, and their as base Malice, by Appealing as a *Roman* to *Cæsar* himself, before whose Authority he also then stood: But he is still kept in Gaol in the same state, to gratifie the Jews, 'till *Agrippa* the *Tetrarch* of *Galilee* came to wait on *Festus*, who (after he had been there some Days) entertain'd him with the Case of St. *Paul*, and acquainted him that he was at a loss what to do with him: He was so Odious to the Jews, that he car'd not to Enlarge him, and so Innocent in himself, that he knew not what Account to send with him to *Rome*: This mov'd | *Agrippa*'s Curiosity to hear him himself; [60] in very great Pomp, he, his Sister, and whole Retinue came to his Tryal: The Apostle made so excellent a Defence, that Mean, Wrong'd, Poor and Unfriended as he was, he was neither Ridiculous or Contemptible to that Courtly Audience, but prevail'd so far upon the Greatest and Wisest Man there, that he forc'd him to declare, *thou hast almost persuaded me to be a Christian*; it would, methinks, be a Sin not to repeat his very handsome Answer.

I would to God, that not only thou, but also all that hear me this day, were not only almost, but altogether such as I am, except these bonds. Acts 26. ver. 29.

His Appeal made it necessary in course of Law, that he should go to *Rome*; in his Passage thither, ver. 23.[1] and in the Tempest, Hunger and Shipwreck, his Constancy was not a Support to him only, but also to the whole Company; and being thrown upon a barbarous Island, he did and receiv'd mutual Offices

---

[1] The correct reference for this passage is Acts 27 and 28. The error was partially corrected in the fourth edition.

among the Poor Savages, not yet cultivated into Ingratitude. At *Rome*, the other Prisoners were carry'd into safe Custody, but he was permitted, with a Soldier only for his Ward, to live in his own hired House, teaching the things which concern the Lord Jesus Christ, no Man forbidding him; for it was only in *Nero*'s Reign, nor had *Rome* | yet arriv'd at the exquisite and refin'd Tyranny of an Inquisition. Thus we have been distinct in running through the more illustrious Passages[a] of this Consummate Life and Character, as they are plac'd in Holy Writ, and may presume, after all the Injuries we have done him, that there is not any Portraiture in the most excellent Writers of Morality, that can come up to its Native Beauty; yet was not he contented to serve his God only, by Example, but has as Eminently done it by Precept; where he pursues Vice, and urges Virtue with all the Reason, Energy and Force that either good Sense or Piety can Inspire: And not upon the airy and fleeting Foundation of the Insensibility noble Minds bear to the Assaults of Fortune; which has been the Impertinence of Heathen Moralists, and[b] among them *Seneca*.

L'Strange's
3*d.* p. *of*
Seneca's
Morals.
Epist. 26.

"A good Man is not only the Friend of God, but "the very Image, the Disciple, the Imitator of him, "and the true Child of his Heav'nly Father: He is "True to himself, and Acts with Constancy and "Resolution. *Scipio*, by a cross Wind being forc'd "into the Power of his Enemies, cast himself upon "the Point of his Sword; and as the People were "enquiring what was become of the General, the "General, says *Scipio*, is very well, and so he Ex-|

[a] passage *o1*[1]   [b] and *add. 10*

The Christian Hero

"pir'd. A Gallant Man, is Fortunes match: His
"Courage Provokes and Despises those terrible Ap-
"pearances, that would Enslave us; a Wise Man is
"out of the reach of Fortune, but not free from the
"Malice of it; and all Attempts upon him are no
"more than *Xerxes*'s Arrows; they may darken the
"Day, but they cannot strike the Sun.

This is *Seneca*'s very Spirit, Opinion and Genius;[a]
but alas, what Absurdity is here! after the Panegyrick
of a Brave or Honest Man, as the Disciple and
Imitator of God, this is Instanc'd in the basest Action
a Man could be guilty of; a General's dispatching
himself in an extream Difficulty, and Deserting his
Men and his Honour; and what is this but doing
a mean Action with a great Countenance? What
could this Imitator of God, out of the Power of
Fortune, do more in Obedience to what they call so,
than Sacrificing his Life to it: But this is Bombast
got into the very Soul, Fustian in thinking!

Quanto Rectius hic qui nil molitur Inepte.

How much better he?

Be ye stedfast, unmoveable, always abounding in the Cor. 15.
Works of the Lord, forasmuch as[b] *you know that your* ver. 58.[1]
Labour is not in vain in the Lord. |

Here is supporting our selves under Misfortunes,
propos'd upon the reasonable terms of Reward and
Punishment; and all other is Fantastick, Arrogant
and Ungrounded.

---

[a] This is *Seneca*'s very Spirit, Opinion and Genius;] This is his very Spirit, Opinion and Genius express'd in better Words than ever he was Master of; 01¹, 01²   [b] as *add.* 01²

---

[1] The correct reference is 1 Cor. 15. 58. The error was corrected in the fourth edition.

The First Epistle to *Corinth* is most exquisitely adapted[a] to the present Temper of *England*, nor did ever that City (tho' proverbial of[b] it) pretend to be more refinedly pleas'd than at present *London*: But St. *Paul* more Emphatically dissuades from those embasing Satisfactions of Sense.

Cor. 9. v. 13.[1] *Meats for the Belly, and the Belly for Meats; but God shall destroy both it and them.*

He, methinks, throws Blush and Confusion in the Face of his Readers, when he Argues on these Subjects; for who can conceive his Body the Mansion of an immortal Spirit, capable to receive the Aspiration and Grace of an Eternal God, and at the same time, by Gluttony and Drunkenness, entertain in that place Fuel to enflame themselves into Adultery, Rage and Revenge? as if our Misery were our Study, and Chastity, Innocence and Temperance, (those easie and agreeable Companions,) were not preferable to the Convulsions of Wrath, and Tortures of Lust.

1. *Cor.* 6 v. 15. [64] *Know ye not that your Bodies are the Members of Christ, shall I then take the | Members of Christ and make them the Members of an Harlot?*

How Ugly has he made *Corinna* at one Sentence? Shall I, who am conscious that he who laid down an immaculate Body, to cleanse me from the Filth and Stain of a Polluted one, and know that the Holy *Jesus* has promis'd to be present to all the Conflicts of my Soul, Banish him thence, and be Guilty of so unnatural a Coition, as to throw

[a] apt *o1¹, o1²* [b] for *o1¹, o1²*

---

[1] The correct reference is 1 Cor. 6. 13. The error was corrected in the fourth edition.

that Temple into the Embraces[a] of a Mercenary Strumpet?

But must we then desert Love and the Fair?
The Cordial Drop Heav'n in our Cup has thrown,
To make the nauseous Draught of Life go down.

No, God forbid! the Apostle allows us a vertuous Enjoyment of our Passions; but indeed extirpates all our false Ideas of Pleasure and Happiness in 'em; he takes Love out of its Disguise, and puts it on its own gay and becoming Dress of Innocence; and indeed it is, among other Reasons, from want of Wit and Invention in our Modern Gallants, that the beautiful Sex is absurdly[b] and vitiously entertain'd by 'em: For there is in their tender Frame, native Simplicity, groundless Fear, and little unaccountable Contradictions, upon which there might be built Expostulations to divert a good and Intelligent young Woman, as well as the fulsome Raptures, guilty Impressions, senseless Deifications, and pretended Deaths that are every Day offer'd her.[1]

No Pen certainly ever surpass'd either the Logick or Rhetorick of his Fifteenth Chapter: How does he intermingle Hope and Fear, Life and Death? Our

---

[a] the Embraces] that Embrace *o1*[1]   the Embrace *o1*[2]
[b] absurdly] so absurdly *o1*[1], *o1*[2]

---

[1] This defence of women foreshadows Steele's interest in the contemporary social problem of feminism. For his discussion of the mind and character of women, see *Lying Lover*, i. 1; *Tatler*, Nos. 53, 149, 172, 201; *Spectator*, Nos. 79, 144; *Guardian*, No. 26. Of the education of women, *Tatler*, Nos. 61, 141, 248; *Spectator*, No. 66; *Guardian*, No. 172. Of courtship and marriage, *Lying Lover*, i. 1; *Tatler*, Nos. 33, 58, 89, 91, 149, 159, 185, 199, and 201; *Spectator*, Nos. 149, 479, 490, 522; *Guardian*, Nos. 5 and 45; *Englishman* (first series), No. 9; *Lover*, No. 24; *Theatre*, No. 6. Of the status of women in society, *Tatler*, No. 49; *Spectator*, No. 342; *Guardian*, No. 15; *Englishman* (first series), No. 9.

rising from our Graves is most admirably Argued on the receiv'd Philosophy, that Corruption precedes Generation, and the easie Instances of new Grain, new Plants and new Trees, from the minute Particles of Seed; and when he has Buried us, how does he move the Heart with an *Oh Death where is thy Sting! Oh Grave where is thy Victory!* We have at once all along the quickest Touches of Distress and of Triumph. It were endless to enumerate these Excellences and Beauties in his Writings; but since they were all in his more publick and ministerial Office, let's see him in his private Life: There is nothing expresses a Man's particular Character more fully, than his Letters to his Intimate Friends; we have one of that Nature of this great Apostle to *Philemon*, which in the Modern Language would perhaps run thus. |

SIR,

"It is with the deepest Satisfaction that I every "Day hear you Commended, for your Generous Be-"haviour to all of that Faith, in the Articles of which "I had the Honour and Happiness to Initiate you; "for which, tho' I might presume to an Authority to "oblige your Compliance in a Request I am going "to make to you, yet chuse I rather to apply my self "to you as a Friend, than an Apostle; for with a Man "of your Great Temper, I know I need not a more "Powerful Pretence than that of my Age and Im-"prisonment: Yet is not my Petition for my self, but "in behalf of the Bearer, your Servant *Onesimus*, who "has robb'd you, and ran away from you; what he "has Defrauded you of, I will be answerable for, this "shall be a Demand upon me; not to say that you

The Christian Hero

"owe me your very self: I call'd him your Servant,
"but he is now also to be Regarded by you in a
"greater Relation, ev'n that of your Fellow-Christian;
"for I esteem him a Son of mine as much as your
"self; nay, methinks it is a certain peculiar Endear-
"ment of him to me, that I had the happiness of
"gaining him in my Confinement: I beseech you | to [67]
"receive him, and think it an Act of Providence, that
"he went away from you for a Season, to return more
"Improv'd to your Service for ever.

This Letter is the sincere Image of a Worthy, Pious, and Brave Man, and the ready Utterance of a generous Christian Temper; How handsomly does he assume, tho' a Prisoner? How humbly condescend, tho' an Apostle? Could any Request have been made, or any Person oblig'd with a better Grace? The very Criminal Servant, is no less with him than his Son and his Brother; for Christianity has that in it, which makes Men pity, not scorn the Wicked, and by a beautiful kind of Ignorance of themselves, think those Wretches their Equals; it aggravates all the Benefits and good Offices of Life, by making 'em seem Fraternal; and the Christian feels the Wants of the Miserable so much his own, that it sweetens the Pain of the oblig'd, when he that gives, does it with an Air, that has neither Oppression or Superiority in it, but had rather have his Generosity appear an enlarg'd Self-Love than diffusive Bounty, and is always a Benefactor with the Mein of a Receiver.

These are the great and beauteous Parts of Life and Friendship; and what is there in all that Morality can prescribe, that can | make a Man do so much as [68] the high Ambition of pleasing his Creator, with whom the Methods of Address are as Immutable as the Favour obtain'd by 'em?

Here, methinks we could begin again upon this Amiable Picture, or shall we search Antiquity for the Period and Consummation of his Illustrious Life, to give him the Crown and Glory of Martyrdom? That were a needless Labour, for he that has been in a Battel, has to his Prince the Merit of having Dy'd there; and St. *Paul* has so often in our Narration confronted Death, that we may bestow upon him that Cœlestial Title, and dismiss him with the just Eulogy in his own spritely Expression that he *Dy'd daily.*

Now the Address and Constancy with which this great Apostle has behav'd himself in so many various Forms of Calamity, are an ample Conviction, that to make our Life one decent and consistent Action, we should have one constant Motive of Living, and that Motive a Confidence in God: For had he Breath'd on any other Cause, instead of Application to the Almighty, he must (on many Occasions which we have mention'd) have ran to the Dagger, or the Bowl of Poison: For the Heathen Virtue prescribes Death before Stripes or Imprisonment; but whatever Pompous Look, Ele|gant Pens may have given to the Illustrious Distress'd (as they would have us think the Persons are,[a] who to evade Miseries, have profus'd their Lives, and rush'd to Death for Relief;) If we look to the bottom of things, we shall easily observe, that 'tis not a generous Scorn of Chains, or delicate Distaste of an Impertinent Being, (which

[a] are, *add. 01*²

two Pretences include all the Varnish that is put upon Self-murder) but[a] it ever was, and ever will be, Pride or Cowardise, that makes Life insupportable: For, since Accidents are not in our Power, but will (in spite of all our Care and Vigilance) befall us; what remains, but that we accommodate our selves so far, as to bear 'em with the greatest Decency and handsomest Patience we are able? And indeed Resistance to what we cannot avoid, is not the Effect of a valiant Heart, but a stubborn Stomach: Which Contumacy, 'till we have quite rooted out our Pride, will always make things too little, and our Cowardise too large: For as Fear gives a false Idea of Sufferings, and Attempts, as above our Strength, tho' they are not such, so Vanity makes things despicable, and beneath us, which are rather for our Honour and Reputation; but if Men would sincerely understand that they are but Creatures, all the distinctions of Great and Little, High and Low, would | be easily swallow'd up in [70] the Contemplation of the Hopes we entertain in the Place we shall have in his Mercy, who is the Author of all things.

CHAP. IV

[b]BUT since we have hitherto treated this Subject in Examples only, (by a View of some Eminent Heathen, by a distant Admiration of the Life of our Blessed Saviour, and a near Examination of that of

[a] but] but that $o1^1$, $o1^2$
[b] *This passage, from the beginning of Chap. IV to* '. . . this World can attack it:' *p. 77, 3rd ed., add. $o1^2$*

70   *The Christian Hero*

his Apostle St. *Paul*,) and since the Indulgence of Mens Passions and Interests calls all things that contradict their Practice, mere Notion, and Theory: We must from[a] this Place descend from the bright Incentives of their Actions to consider Lower Life, and talk of Motives which are common to all Men, and which are the Impulses of the ordinary World, as well as of Captains, Heroes, Worthies, Lawgivers, and Saints. Which when we have perform'd, if it shall appear, that those Motives are best us'd and improv'd, when join'd with Religion; we may rest assur'd, that it is a Stable, Sober, and Practical, as well as Generous, Exalted and Heroick, Position, that True Greatness of Mind is to be maintain'd only by Christian Principles. |

[71] We will venture then to assert, that the two great Springs of Human Actions are Fame and Conscience; for tho' we usually say such a one does not value his Reputation, and such a one is a Man of no Conscience, it will perhaps be very easie to prove, that there seldom[b] lives a Person so Profligate and Abandon'd, as not to prefer either the One or the[c] Other, even to Life its self; and by the way, methinks, the quick Pleasure Men taste in the one, and as lively Smart in the other, are strong Arguments of their Immortal Nature: For such Abstracted Sufferings and Enjoyments argue our Souls too large for their present Mansions, and raise Us (ev'n while we are in these Bodies) to a Being which does not at all affect 'em, but which is wholly Spiritual and Immaterial.

So strong (as we were going to proceed) is the

[a] in *01*2   [b] seldom] seldom ever *01*2   [c] the *add. 10*

The Christian Hero

Passion for Fame,[1] that it never seems utterly extinct: For not to look among the Men of the Sword, (whose whole Pay it is,) and who suffer infinite Hazards, Toils, and Miseries to enjoy it; not, I say, to dwell upon them, whose more professed Pursuit is Glory, we shall find it Intrudes also as restlessly upon those of the Quill, nay the very Authors who conceal their Names, are yet Vainer than they who publish theirs. They both indeed aim at your Applause, but | the [72] Mock-Disguise of themselves in the former, is but a more subtle Arrogance, at once to enjoy your Esteem, and the Reputation of Contemning it: Nay, not only such who would recommend themselves by Great Actions, and Liberal Arts, but ev'n the lowest of Mankind, and they who have gone out of the road, not only of Honour, but also common Honesty, have still a remaining relish for Praise and Applause. For you may frequently observe Malefactors at an Execution, ev'n in that Weight of Shame and Terror, preserve as it were a corner of their Souls for the Reception of Pity, and Dye with the sturdy Satisfaction of not appearing to bend at the Calamity, or perhaps desert their Accomplices, by the Sacrifice and Betraying of whose Lives we frequently see they might have sav'd their Own.

By which last Instance (that the basest Men have still something Punctilious to 'em) we may Observe, that the Sense of Fame and Conscience is never quite Kill'd, but that when we are come to the worst, we have only carry'd 'em into another Interest, and

---

[1] For Steele's detailed discussions of the passion for fame, see *Tatler*, Nos. 68 and 77; *Spectator*, Nos. 38, 97, 172, and 188; *Guardian*, No. 1; *Englishman* first series), Nos. 10 and 48.

turn'd our Gratifications that way, only to different Objects; nor can it be imagin'd that the Love-Histories we daily hear young Fellows relate of the Favours and Fondness of Debauch'd Women to 'em, can be all that time design'd for a Self-Accusation: No, their idle Minds have only shifted their Sense of things, and tho' they Glory in their Shame, yet still they Glory.

What then must Men do to make themselves easie in this Invincible Passion, or how shall they possess a thing that is of so Inconsistent a Nature, that if they will be Masters of it, they must shun it: For if they speak to their own Advantage, or suffer another to do it to 'em, they are equally Contemptible: Thus they spend their Lives in pursuit of *an ever absent Good*; and yet, tho' Applause must never come quite Home to 'em, they are it seems miserable, except they are conscious that they have it.

Now if every Heart lies open to it, that Heart that is most Passionate of it,[1] must be in eternal Anxiety to attain it, though that very Love[a] frequently leads to the Loss of it: For when our utmost Bliss is plac'd in this Charming Possession of Praise, and the World's Opinion of our Accomplishments, a Flatterer needs no more in Attempts upon Mens Honesty, and Womens Chastity, but their being convinc'd their Crimes may be a Secret: So easily, alas! are both Sexes led by admiration into Contempt.

To Rectifie therefore, and Adjust our Desires in this kind, we have the other con|comitant Motive of a[b] Living Conscience, or the Knowledge and

[a] Love] Love of it *01*²   [b] a *add. 10*

[1] See 'A Note on the Text', p. xxxi, n. 2.

The Christian Hero

Judgment of what we are doing, which in the Voyage of Life is our Ballast, as the other is our Sail: But tho' Fame and Conscience, like Judge and Criminal, are thus plac'd together in us, they will have an Understanding, and go into each others Interest, except there is a Superior Court, in which both may be Examin'd. Here was the unhappy Block on which the noble Heathen stumbled, and lost his way; for the bare Conscience of a thing's being ill, was not of Consideration enough of its self to support Men in the Anguish of Disgrace, Poverty and Imprisonment. But Success, Applause, Renown, Honour and Command had Attractions too forcible to mere Men, to be relinquish'd but with Life it self; to which Truth, the braver and higher Part of the Heathen World have Dy'd Martyrs.

The different Sects and sortings of themselves into distinct Classes of Opinion, seem to be no other than the Prosecution of this Natural Impulse to Reputation, which Class was Stoical or *Epicurean*, or the like,[a] according to the force and bent of their Complexions, which they mis-understood for their Conscience; and *Salust* begins his fine Story of *Catiline*'s Conspiracy, with an acknowledgement to this Purpose, for he takes | it to be the peculiar Duty and [75] Superiority of the Human Race above other Animals (which he calls Prone and Obedient to their Bellies) *Ne Vitam silentio Transeant*, not to let Life pass away in a Lazy Silence; and further, *Is mihi Demum vivere & frui Anima videtur qui, negotio aliquo intentus Artis, bonæ famam quærit:* He only in his Opinion might truly be said to *Live*, who being employ'd in some

[a] or the like,] and so forth *or*²

useful Affair, obtain'd a Reputation in an Honest or Liberal Art. Thus this Author of Sober and Excellent Sense, makes it the End and Happy Consummation of a well-spent Life, to arrive at a good Fame; which makes our Assertion in the beginning of this Discourse very Natural, *viz.* That the Heathen Virtues, which were little else but Disguis'd or Artificial Passions, (since their Good was in Fame) must rise or fall with Disappointment or Success.

Now our good God, who claims not an utter Extirpation, but the Direction only of our Passions, has provided also for this great Desire, in giving it a Scope as boundless as it self; and since 'tis never to be Satisfy'd, hath[a] allow'd it an Aim which may supply it with Eternal employment.

Matt.5. 16. *Let your Light so shine before Men that they may see your Good Works, and Glorifie your Father which is in Heaven.* |

[76] In this Command is the whole Business of Reputation, (about which we are so miserably Anxious) wholly rectify'd; and Fame no longer a Turbulent, Wayward, Uneasie Pursuit, but (when thus made a Subordinate, and Secondary Cause of Action) a calm, easie, indifferent and untroubled Possession.

And what more glorious Ambition can the Mind of Man have, than to consider it self actually Imploy'd in the Service of, and in a manner[b] in Conjunction with, the Mind of the Universe, which is for ever Busie without Toil, and Working without Weariness.

Thus the Spirit of Man, by new Acquisitions, will daily receive Earnests of a nobler State, and by its

---

a hath *add.* *10*   b kind *or2*

The Christian Hero

own enlargement better apprehend that Spirit, after whose Image it was made, which knows no confinement of Place.

This adjusted Passion will make Men truly Agreeable, substantially Famous, for when the first Intention pursues the Service of the Almighty, distinction will naturally come, the only way it ever does come, without being apparently Courted; nor will Men be Lost through a fondness of it, by affectation in the familiar Life, or Knavery in the Busie: |

It is not a Stoical Rant, but a reasonable Confidence in a Man thus Arm'd, to be unmov'd at Misfortunes; let the Sea, or the People rage; let the Billows beat, the World be confus'd, the Earth be shook; 'Tis not to him a Terror, but a daily request of his to hasten the very last Day of Human Nature, that He may finish this various Being, and enjoy the Presence of his Maker in an endless Tranquility.

Thus, by taking in Fame, the Christian Religion (and no other Motive) has fortify'd our Minds on all sides, and made 'em Impregnable by any Happiness or Misery with which this World can attack it:[a] And now, if it is Impartially apparent to us, that the Christian Scheme is not only the way to Ease and Composure of Mind in unhappy Circumstances, but also the noblest Spur to honest and great Actions, what hinders, but that we be Baptiz'd, and Resolve all our perplex'd Notions of Justice, Generosity, Patience and Bravery, into that one easie and portable Virtue, Piety? Which could arm our Ancestors in this Faith with so resistless[b] and victorious a Con-

[77]

---

[a] *The passage from the beginning of Chap. IV to this point was added in* 01^2
[b] resistless 01^1, 01^2 *Misprinted* restless *10*

stancy, that by their Sufferings, their Religion, from the Outcast and Scorn of the Earth, has ascended Soveraign Thrones; and Defender of the Faith, and most Christian King, are Appellations of the Great-[78] est Monarchs of | the most refin'd Nations; nor can we enough thank the Almighty, who has dispos'd us into the World, when the Christian Name bears Pomp and Authority, and not in its offensive, low and despis'd Beginnings: But alas! its State is[a] as much Militant as ever, for there are Earthly and Narrow Souls, as deeply Scandal'd at the Prosperity the Professors and Teachers of this Sacred Faith enjoy, and object to 'em the Miseries and Necessities of the Primitive Believers: Light and Superficial Men! Not seeing that Riches is a much more dangerous Dispensation than that of[b] Poverty, this we Oppose as a Foe, that we run to meet as a Friend, and an Enemy does his Work more successfully in an Embrace than a Blow; but since the Necessaries, Conveniencies and Honours of Life which the Clergy enjoy, are so great an Offence to their Despisers, they are the more engag'd to hold 'em dear; for they who envy a Man for what he has, would certainly scorn him without it; when therefore they are both in good and bad Fortune irreconcilable to 'em, may they always offend with their Happiness; for it is not to be doubted, but that there are Bishops and Governors in the Church of *England*, whose decent Hospitality, Meekness, [79] and Charity to their Brethren, will place 'em in | the same Mansions with the most Heroick Poor; and convince the Mistake of their Enemies, that the Eternal Pastor has giv'n his Worldly Blessings into

---

[a] is] is now *o1*[1], *o1*[2]   [b] under *o1*[1], *o1*[2]

The Christian Hero

Hands by which he approves their Distribution; and still bestows upon us great and exemplary Spirits, that can Conquer the Difficulties and Enchantments of Wealth it self.

To follow such excellent Leaders, it will be necessary we now consider also, what may be our best Rule in that State we call our good Fortune; and enquire whether Christianity can as well become its Professors in the Enjoyments of Prosperity, as we have seen it has in the hardships of Adversity; this also we shall best know by contemplating our Natural Frame and Tendency, which Religion either assists or corrects in these Circumstances.

The Eternal God, in whom we Live, and Move, and have our Being, has Impress'd upon us all one Nature, which as an Emanation from him, who is Universal Life, presses us by Natural Society to a close Union with each other; which is, methinks, a sort of Enlargement of our very selves when we run into the Ideas, Sensations and Concerns of our Brethren: By this Force of their Make, Men are insensibly hurried into each other, and by a secret Charm we lament with the Unfortunate, | and rejoice [80] with the Glad; for it is not possible for an human Heart to be averse to any thing that is Human: But by the very Mein and Gesture of the Joyful and Distress'd we rise and fall into their Condition; and since Joy is Communicative, 'tis reasonable that Grief should be Contagious, both which are seen and felt at a look, for one Man's Eyes are Spectacles to another to Read his Heart: Those useful and honest Instruments do not only discover Objects to us, but make our selves also Transparent; for they, in spite of

Dissimulation, when the Heart is full, will brighten into Gladness, and gush into Tears: From this Foundation in nature is kindled that noble Spark of Cœlestial Fire, we call Charity or Compassion, which opens our Bosoms, and extends our Arms to Embrace all Mankind, and by this it is that the Amorous Man is not more suddenly melted with Beauty, than the Compassionate with Misery.

Thus are we fram'd for mutual Kindness, good Will and Service, and therefore our Blessed Saviour has been pleased to give us (as a reiterated Abridgment of all his Law) the Command of Loving one another; and the Man that Imbibes that noble Principle is in no Danger of insolently Transgressing against his Fellow Creatures, but will certainly use [81] all the Advantages | which he has from Nature and Fortune to the Good and Welfare of others, for whose Benefit (next to the Adoration of his Maker) he knows he was Created: This Temper of Mind, when neither Polluted or Mis-led, tends to this Purpose, and the Improvement of it by Religion raises on it an exalted Superstructure, which inclines him in his Words and Actions, to be above the little Crafts and Doubles with which the World beneath him is perplex'd: He is Intrinsically possessed of what mere Morality must own to be a Fantastical Chimæra, the being wholly dis-interested in the Affairs of the Person he affects or befriends; for indeed when the Regard of our Maker is not our first Impulse and Desire in our Hopes and Purposes, it is impossible but that the Fondness of our selves and our own Interest must recurr upon us, and leaven the whole Course of our Actions: When the Fountain is Muddy it must stain the Rivulet, and the prædominant Passion gives a Tincture to all our Cares and Pleasures; so that Men ordinarily Love others out of a Tenderness to themselves, and do good Offices to receive 'em with Encrease and Usury: Nay, if we follow the best Friendship we meet with to its Sourse, and allow it to be what it sometimes really is, a passionate Inclina|tion to [82] serve another, without hopes or visible Possibility of receiving a Return, yet we must also allow, that there is a deep Interest to our selves (though indeed a Beautiful one) in satisfying that Inclination; but that good Intention is subject to be Chang'd and Interrupted (as perhaps it was taken up) by Accident, Mistake, or turn of Humour; but he that Loves others for the Love of God, must be unchangeable, for the Cause of his Benevolence to us is so; and though indeed he is not without Self-regard in the hopes of receiving one Day an immense Reward of all his Labour, yet since that is separate from this World, it is to all Intents of Life, as far from the Interfering with our Purposes, as if he had no such Expectation; and that very Prospect in him is not of a selfish incommunicable Nature, but is augmented and furthered by our Participation, while his Joys are quickened and redoubled by the joint Wishes of others: This is that Blessed State of Mind which is so excellently call'd Singleness of Heart; which inseparable Peace and Happiness, 'tis not in the power of all the Tinsel in the World to discompose; for to a Christian and knowing Mind Earth is but Earth, though the refin'd Dirt shine into Gems, and glister into Gold. |

[83] He that thus justly values the Wealth which Heav'n has bestow'd upon him, cannot grow giddy in the Possession of it, for it serves only to express a Noble and Christian Nature, which dispenses liberally, and enjoys abstinently the Goods which he knows he may lose and must leave: But this extensive Magnanimity, according to the Rules of our Faith, is not to be bestow'd on those only who are our Friends, but must reach also to[a] our very Enemies; though[b] good Sense as well as Religion is so utterly banish'd the World, that Men glory in their very Passions, and pursue Trifles with the utmost Vengeance:[1] So little do they know that to Forgive is the most arduous Pitch human Nature can arrive at; a Coward has often Fought, a Coward has often Conquer'd, but *a Coward never Forgave*. The Power of doing that flows from a Strength of Soul conscious of its own Force, whence it draws a certain Safety which its Enemy is not of consideration enough to Interrupt; for 'tis peculiar in the Make of a brave Man to have his Friends seem much above him, his Enemies much below him.

Yet though the neglect of our Enemies may so intense a Forgiveness, as the Love of 'em is not to be in the least accounted for by the force of Con-
[84] stitution, but is a more | spiritual and refin'd Moral

[a] to *add. 10* [b] but *o1*

---

[1] This somewhat veiled invective against duelling was the first of a long series of attacks made by Steele during the next two decades. In the *Lying Lover* (1703) the duel was a culminating episode, used as the basis for a moral lecture. See, also, for further discussion of duelling by Steele, *Tatler*, Nos. 25, 26, 28, 29, 31, 39; *Spectator*, Nos. 84 and 97; *Guardian*, Nos. 20, 129, 133; *Theatre*, Nos. 19 and 26. The duelling episode in the *Conscious Lovers* (1722), for which Steele declared he wrote the play, demonstrated that a man of honour could honourably refuse a challenge.

The Christian Hero

introduc'd by him, who Dy'd for those that Persecuted him, yet very justly deliver'd to us, when we consider our selves as Offenders, and to be forgiven on the reasonable Terms of Forgiving; For who can ask what he will not bestow? Especially when that Gift is attended with a Redemption from the cruellest Slavery to the most acceptable Freedom: For when the Mind is in the Contemplation of Revenge, all its Thoughts must surely be Tortur'd with the Alternate Pangs of Rancour, Envy, Hatred, and Indignation: And they who profess a Sweet in the Enjoyment of it, certainly never felt the consummate Bliss of Reconciliation: At such an Instant the false Ideas we receiv'd unravel, and the Shiness, the Distrust, the secret Scorns, and all the base Satisfactions, Men had in each others Faults and Misfortunes, are dispell'd, and their Souls appear in their Native Whiteness, without the least Streak of that Malice or Distaste which sullied 'em: And perhaps those very Actions, which (when we look'd at 'em in the oblique Glance with which Hatred doth always see[a] Things) were Horrid and Odious, when observ'd with honest and open Eyes, are Beauteous and Ornamental. |

But if Men are averse to us in the most violent Degree, and we can never bring 'em to an amicable Temper, then indeed we are to exert an obstinate Opposition to 'em, and never let the Malice of our Enemies have so effectual an Advantage over us, as to escape our good Will: For the neglected and despised Tenets of Religion are so Generous, and in so Transcendent and Heroick a manner disposed for publick Good, that 'tis not in a Man's power to avoid

---

[a] doth always see] always sees or^1, or^2

their Influence; for the Christian is as much inclin'd to your Service when your Enemy, as the moral Man when your Friend.

Now since the Dictates of Christianity are thus excellently suited to an enlarg'd Love and Ambition to serve the World, the most immediate Method of seeing to what height they would accomplish that noble Work, is taking the Liberty of observing how they would naturally Influence the Actions and Passions of such Persons, as have Power to exert all the Dictates and Impulses which are Inspir'd, either by their Inclinations or Opinions; for whatever is Acted in the narrow Path of a private Life, passes away in the same Obscurity that 'twas perform'd in[a]; while the Purposes and Conduct of Princes attract all Eyes, and employ all Tongues; in which difficult Station and Character it is not pos|sible, but that a Man, without Religion must be more exquisitely Unhappy,[b] than the meanest of his Vassals; for the repeated Pomp and Pageantry of Greatness must needs become in time, either Languid in the Satisfactions they give, or turn the Heads of the Powerful, so that 'tis absolutely necessary that he should have something of more inward and deep regard, to keep his Condition from being an Oppression, either to himself or others.

There were not ever before the Entrance of the Christian Name into the World, Men who have maintain'd a more renown'd Carriage than the two great Rivals who possess the full Fame of the present Age, and will be the Theme and Examination of the future: They are exactly formed by Nature for those

[a] in *add.* 01² [b] *Misprinted* Happy, 10

The Christian Hero

Ends, to which Heav'n seems to have sent 'em amongst us: Both animated with a restless Desire of Glory, but pursue it by different Means, and with different Motives: To one it consists in an extensive undisputed Empire over his Subjects, to the other in their rational and voluntary Obedience: One's Happiness is founded in their want of Power, the others in their want of Desire to oppose him: The one enjoys the Summet of Fortune with the Luxury of a *Persian*, the other with the Moderation of a *Spartan*; one | is made to Oppress, the other to relieve the Oppressed: The one is satisfied with the Pomp and Ostentation of Power to prefer and debase his Inferiors, the other delighted only with the Cause and Foundation of it, to cherish and protect 'em: To one therefore Religion is[a] but a convenient Disguise, to the other a vigorous Motive of Action.

For without such Tyes of real and solid Honour, there is no way of forming a Monarch, but after the *Machiavilian* Scheme, by which a Prince must ever seem to have all Vertues, but really to be Master of none, but is to be Liberal, Merciful and Just, only as they serve his Interests; while with the noble Art of Hypocrisie, Empire would be to be Extended, and new Conquests be made by new Devices, by which prompt Address his Creatures might insensibly give Law in the Business of Life, by leading Men in the Entertainment of it, and making their great Monarch the Fountain of all that's delicate and refin'd, and his Court the Model for Opinions in Pleasure, as well as the Pattern in Dress; which might prevail so far upon an undiscerning World as (to accomplish it for

[a] is] would be *o1*[1]

its approaching Slavery) to make it receive a superfluous Babble for an Universal Language. |

Thus when Words and Show are apt to pass for the substantial Things they[a] are only to express, there would need no more to enslave a Country but to adorn a Court; for while every Man's Vanity makes him believe himself capable of becoming Luxury, Enjoyments are a ready Bait for Sufferings, and the hopes of Preferment Invitations to Servitude, which Slavery would be colour'd with all the Agreements, as they call it, Imaginable: The noblest Arts and Artists, the finest Pens and most elegant Minds, jointly employ'd to set it off, with the various Embellishments of sumptuous Entertainments, charming Assemblies and polish'd Discourses: And those apostate Abilities of Men, the ador'd Monarch might profusely and skilfully encourage, while they flatter his Virtue, and gild his Vice at so high a rate, that he without Scorn of the one, or Love of the other, would alternately and occasionally use both, so that his Bounty should support him in his Rapines, his Mercy in his Cruelties.

Nor is it to give Things a more severe Look than is natural, to suppose such must be the Consequences of a Prince's having no other Pursuit than that of his own Glory; for if we consider an Infant born into the World, and beholding it self the mightiest Thing in it, it self the present Admira|tion and future Prospect of a fawning People, who profess themselves great or mean according to the Figure he is to make amongst 'em, what Fancy would not be Debauch'd to believe they were but what they professed them-

[a] *Misprinted* we *10*

The Christian Hero

selves, his mere Creatures, and use 'em as such by purchasing with their Lives a boundless Renown, which he, for want of a more just Prospect, would place in the number of his Slaves,[a] and the extent of his Territories; such undoubtedly would be the Tragical Effects of a Prince's living with no Religion, which are not to be surpass'd but by his having a False one.

If Ambition were Spirited with Zeal, what would follow, but that his People should be converted into an Army, whose Swords can make Right in Power, and solve Controversie in Belief; and if Men should be Stiff-necked to the Doctrine of that visible Church, let 'em be contented with an Oar and a Chain in the midst of Stripes and Anguish, to contemplate on him, whose Yoke is Easie, and whose Burthen is Light.

With a Tyranny begun on his own Subjects, and Indignation that others draw their Breath Independent of his Frown or Smile, why should he not proceed to the seizure of the World; and if nothing but the Thirst of Sway were the Motive | of his Actions, [90] why should Treaties be other than mere Words, or solemn National Compacts be any thing but an Halt in the March of[b] that Army, who are never to lay down their Arms, 'till all Men are reduc'd to the Necessity of Hanging their Lives on his Way-ward Will; who might Supinely, and at Leisure, expiate his own Sins by other Mens Sufferings; while he daily Meditates New Slaughter, and New Conquest.

For mere Man, when giddy with unbridled Power, is an insatiate Idol, not to be appeased with Myriads

[a] his Slaves] *Misprinted* Slaves, *10*   [b] *Misprinted* in *10*

offer'd to his Pride, which may be puffed up by the Adulation of a base and prostrate World, into an Opinion that he is something more than Human, by being something less: And alas, what is there that Mortal Man will not believe of himself, when Complimented with the Attributes of God? He can then conceive Thoughts of a Power as *Omnipræsent* as his: But should there be such a Foe of Mankind now upon Earth, have our Sins so far provok'd Heav'n, that we are left utterly Naked to his Fury? Is there no Power, no Leader, no Genius that can Conduct and Animate us to our Death, or our Defence? Yes, our great God never gave one to Reign by his Permission, but he gave to another also, to Reign by his Grace. |

[91] All the Circumstances of the Illustrious Life of our Prince seem to have Conspir'd to make him the Check and Bridle of Tyranny, for his Mind has been strengthen'd and confirm'd by one continued Struggle, and Heav'n has Educated him by Adversity to a quick Sense of the Distresses and Miseries of Mankind, which he was born to Redress: In just Scorn of the trivial Glories and light Ostentations of Power, that Glorious Instrument of Providence, moves like that, in a steddy, calm and silent Course, Independent either of Applause or of Calumny, which renders him, if not in a Political, yet in a Moral, a Philosophick, an Heroick, and a Christian Sense, an absolute Monarch: Who satisfied with this unchangeable, just and ample Glory, must needs turn all his Regards from himself, to the Service of others; for he begins his Enterprizes with his own share in the Success of 'em, for Integrity bears in its self its

The Christian Hero

Reward, nor can that which depends not on Event ever know Disappointment.

With the undoubted Character of a glorious Captain, and (what he much more Values than the most splendid Titles) that of a sincere and honest Man, he is the Hope and Stay of *Europe*, an Universal Good not to be Engrossed by us only; for di|stant Poten- [92] tates implore his Friendship, and injur'd Empires Court his Assistance: He rules the World, not by an Invasion of the People of the Earth, but the Address of its Princes; and if that World should be again rous'd from the Repose which his prevailing Arms have giv'n it, why should we not hope that there is an Almighty, by whose Influence the terrible Enemy that thinks himself prepar'd for Battel, may find he is but ripe for Destruction, and that there may be in the Womb of Time great Incidents, which may make the Catastrophe of a prosperous Life as Unfortunate, as the particular Scenes of it were Successful.

For there does not want a skilful Eye, and resolute Arm, to observe and grasp the Occasion: A Prince, who from a just Notion of his Duty to that Being, to whom he must be accountable, has in the service of his Fellow-Creatures, a noble contempt of Pleasures, and Patience of Labours, to whom 'tis Hæreditary to be the Guardian and Asserter of the Native Rights and Liberties of Mankind; and who, with a rational Ambition, knows how much greater 'tis to give than take away; whose every Day is productive of some great Action, in behalf of Mens Universal Liberty, which great Affection to 'em 'tis not in the | Power [93] of their very Ingratitude to alienate; he is Constant and Collected in himself, nor can their Murmurs interrupt his Toil, any more than their Dreams his Vigilance; a Prince, who never did or spoke any thing that could justly give Grief to his People, but when he mention'd his *Succession* to 'em: But what grateful Mind can bear that insupportable Reflection? No, we will with endless Adoration implore Heav'n to continue him to us, or expire in Heaps before his Pavilion, to guard his important Life, and in the Joint Cause of Heav'n and Earth, our Religion and our Liberty, destroy like Ministring Angels, or die an Army of Martyrs.

FINIS

BIBLIOGRAPHY[1]

TWENTY-TWO editions of the *Christian Hero* are evidence of its vogue from 1701 to 1820. In every decade but one of the eighteenth century there were one or more editions, and there were four in the first quarter of the nineteenth. In Steele's lifetime nine editions and a French translation were published, four editions appearing between 1710 and 1712 during the run of the *Tatler* and the *Spectator*; and nine more came out between 1729, the year of his death, and 1800. Of these twenty-two editions, fourteen were published in London—eleven by Tonson; one each in Oxford, Berwick, Whitehaven, and Bungay; two in Dublin; and two in the United States.

1701 (April)

The / Christian / Hero: / An / *Argument* / Proving That / No Principles but those of / Religion are sufficient to make a / Great Man. / [rule] / —— *Fragili quærens illidere dentem* / *Offendet sido* [*sic*] —— Ho. / [rule] / London, / Printed for *Jacob Tonson*, within *Gray's-Inn-* / *Gate*, next *Gray's-* / *Inn-* / *Lane*. 1701. /

The title-page is enclosed within a double-rule frame.
Octavo.

---

[1] An adequate bibliography of the *Christian Hero* has been lacking. The lists of editions given by Watt, Darling, Lowndes, and Allibone are incomplete and in some cases inaccurate. The hand-lists made by Edward Solly (*The Antiquary*, xii (1885), 233) and by George A. Aitken (*ibid.*, xiii (1886), 38) have gaps; and even Aitken's final list compiled for his *Life of Richard Steele* (1889. See Appendix V (ii. 390)) is deficient. The present bibliography aims at completeness. It includes a description of every discoverable edition, with such particulars as will enable them to be identified and with a census of the libraries in Great Britain and the United States where copies may be found.

This bibliography is reprinted from the *Transactions of the Bibliographical Society*, x (June, 1929).

Signatures: A–G in eights.

Pagination: Pp. [i, ii], List of books printed for Jacob Tonson; p. [iii], title; p. [iv], blank; pp. [v–x], Dedication to Lord Cutts; pp. [xi–xvi], Preface; pp. 1–95, text; p. [96], blank. 'Finis' on p. 95. A double-rule heading for the Dedication, the Preface, and [Chap. I].[1]

Advertised in the *Post Boy*, 15–17 April 1701.

Copies at University of Texas Library, Aitken Collection* and Wrenn Collection; Harvard College Library; Henry E. Huntington Library; British Museum; Bodleian Library; Cambridge University Library.

1701 (July)

The / Christian / Hero: / An / *Argument* / Proving That / *No Principles but those of* / Religion / Are sufficient to make a Great Man. / [rule] / —— *Fragili quærens illidere dentem* / *Offendet solido* —— Ho. / [rule] / Second Edition, with Additions. / [rule] / *London*, / Printed for *Jacob Tonson*, within *Gray's-Inn-* / *Gate*, next *Gray's-Inn-Lane*, 1701. /

The title-page is enclosed within a double-rule frame.

Octavo.

Signatures: A five leaves. B–G in eights. H three leaves.

Pagination: P. [i], Title; p. [ii], blank; pp. [iii–vi], Dedication to Lord Cutts; pp. [vii–x], Preface; pp. 1–102, text. 'Finis' on p. 102. A double-rule heading for the Dedication, the Preface, and [Chap. I.]. Chap. IV is misprinted Chap. VI (p. 78).

Advertised in the *Post Boy*, 17–19 July 1701.

Copies at University of Texas Library, Aitken Collection* and Wrenn Collection; Yale University Library; British Museum; Victoria and Albert Museum, Dyce Collection, autographed copy.

1710 (November)

The / Christian Hero: / An / Argument / Proving that no / Principles / But Those Of / *Religion* / Are Sufficient to make a / Great Man. / [rule] / —— *Fragili quærens illidere dentem* / *Offendet solido* —— Ho. / [rule] / The Third Edition. / [rule] / *London*: /

---

[1] The copy described is starred.

Bibliography

Printed for *Jacob Tonson*, within *Gray's-Inn Gate*, | next *Gray's-Inn-Lane*. 1710. |

Octavo.
Signatures: A–F in eights, G four leaves.
Pagination: P. [i], Title; p. [ii], blank; pp. [iii–vi], Dedication to Lord Cutts; pp. [vii–x], Preface; pp. [1] and 2–93, text; p. [94], blank. 'Finis' on p. 93. A double-rule heading for the Dedication, the Preface, and [Chap. I.].
Advertised in the *London Gazette*, 7–9 November 1710.

Copies at University of Texas Library, Aitken Collection;* University of Chicago Library; Cambridge University Library.

1711 (April)

The | Christian Hero: | An | Argument | Proving that no | Principles | But those of | *Religion* | Are sufficient to make a Great Man. | [rule] | Written by Mr. Steele. | [rule] | —— *Fragili quærens illidere dentem* | *Offendet solido* —— Ho. | [rule] | The Fourth Edition. | [rule] | London: | Printed for *J. T.* and Sold by *O. Lloyd*, | near the Church in the *Temple*. 1711.

Duodecimo.
Signatures: One unsigned leaf, A–C in twelves, D six leaves.
Pagination: P. [i], blank; p. [ii], advertisement consisting of a list of books sold by O. Lloyd; p. [iii], Title; p. [iv], blank; pp. [v–x], Dedication to Lord Cutts; pp. [xi–xvi], Preface; pp. [1] and 2–70, text. 'Finis' on p. 70. Head ornaments and ornamental initials at the beginning of the Dedication, the Preface, and each chapter. Tail ornaments following the Dedication and Chap. II.

The copy described (in Columbia University Library) is bound in modern binding with the fourth volume of the *Tatler: The Lucubrations of Isaac Bickerstaff Esq. Revised and Corrected by the Author*, vol. iv., London, Printed and Sold by Charles Lillie ... and John Morphew. MDCCXI.

The advertisement for this edition in the *Daily Courant*, 19 April 1711, states that it is printed in 'a neat Pocket Volume so as to be bound up with the 4th Volume of the Tatlers'.

Copies at Columbia University Library;* Library Company of Philadelphia (bound singly in modern binding); British Museum.

1711 (December)

The / Christian Hero: / An / Argument / Proving that no / Principles / But those of / *Religion* / Are Sufficient to make a / Great Man. / [rule] / Written by Mr. *Steele*. / [rule] / ——— *Fragili quærens illidere dentem* / *Offendet solido* ——— Ho. / [rule] / The Fifth Edition. / [rule] / *London*: / Printed for *J. T.* And sold by *Owen* / *Lloyd* near the Church in the *Temple*. / MDCCXI. /

Duodecimo.

Signatures: A–C in twelves (A1 missing), D six leaves.

Pagination: P. [i], Title; p. [ii], blank; pp. [iii–viii], Dedication to Lord Cutts; pp. [ix–xiv], Preface; pp. [1] and 2–68, text. 'Finis' on p. 68. Head ornaments and ornamental initials at the beginning of the Dedication, the Preface, and each chapter. Tail ornament following the Preface.

Advertised in the *Post Boy*, 6–8 December 1711.

Copies at University of Texas Library, Aitken Collection;* Harvard College Library; Yale University Library; British Museum; Bodleian Library.

1712 (November)

The / Christian Hero: / An / Argument / Proving that no / Principles / But those of / *Religion* / Are Sufficient to make a / Great Man. / [rule] / Written by Mr. *Steele*. / [rule] / ——— *Fragili quærens illidere dentem* / *Offendet solido* ——— Ho. / [rule] / The Sixth Edition. / [rule] / *London*: / Printed for *Jacob Tonson* at *Shakespear's* / *Head* over-against *Catherine Street* in / the *Strand*. 1712. /

Duodecimo.

Signatures: A six leaves, B–D in twelves.

Pagination: P. [i], blank; p. [ii], advertisement consisting of a list of books printed for Jacob Tonson; p. [iii], Title; p. [iv], blank; pp. [v–x], Dedication to Lord Cutts; pp. [xi–xvi], Preface; pp. [1] and 2–68, text. 'Finis' on p. 68. Head ornaments and ornamental initials at the beginning of the Dedication, the Preface, and each chapter. Tail ornament following the Preface. (Ornaments slightly different in design from those of the fifth edition.)

Advertised in the *Spectator*, 29 November 1712.

Copies at University of Texas Library, Aitken Collection;*
British Museum; Cambridge University Library.

1722

The / Christian Hero: / An / Argument / Proving that no / Principles / But those of / *Religion* / Are sufficient to make a / Great Man. / [rule] / By Sir *Richard Steele*. / [rule] / —— *Fragili quærens illidere dentem* / *Offendet solido* —— Hor. / [rule] / The Seventh Edition. / [rule] / *London*: / Printed for Jacob Tonson at *Shake-* / *spear's Head* over-against *Catherine Street* / in the *Strand*. / MDCCXXII. /

Duodecimo.
Signatures: A–C in twelves, D six leaves.
Pagination: P. [i], Title; p. [ii], blank; pp. [iii–ix], Dedication to Lord Cutts; p. [x], blank; pp. [xi–xvi], Preface; pp. [1] and 2–68, text. 'Finis' on p. 68. Head ornaments and ornamental initials at the beginning of the Dedication, the Preface, and each chapter. Tail ornament following the Preface. (All ornaments more elaborate than those in the fifth and sixth editions.)

Copies at University of Texas Library, Aitken Collection;* Harvard College Library; Massachusetts Historical Society; British Museum; Bodleian Library.

1725

The / *Christian Hero*: / An Argument proving that no / Principles / But those of / Religion / Are Sufficient / To make a Great Man. / [rule] / By Sir *Richard Steele*. / [rule] / —— *Fragili quærens illidere dentem* / *Offendet solido* —— Hor. / [rule] / [ornament] / [rule] / *Dublin*: / Printed by S. Powell, for George Risk at the Cor- / ner of *Castle-lane* in *Dame's-street*, near the *Horse-guard*, / MDCCXXV. /

The title-page is printed in black and red.
Octavo.
Signatures: A–D in eights, [E] one leaf.
Pagination: P. [i], Title; p. [ii], blank; pp. [iii–vi], Dedication to Lord Cutts; pp. [vii–x], Preface; pp. [1] and 2–55, text; p. [56], blank. 'Finis' on p. 55. Ornamental initials at the beginning of the

Dedication, the Preface, and [Chap. I.]. Head ornaments for the Dedication, the Preface, and each chapter. Tail ornaments following the Preface and 'Finis'.

In the copy described (in Columbia University Library), the *Christian Hero* is the first item in a volume (modern binding) containing the following:

(2) Combe, Edward, *The Art of Being Easy at All Times and in all Places*, Dublin, 1725.

(3) ———, *A Faithful and Exact Narrative of the Horrid Tragedy Lately Acted at the Thorn in Polish Prussia* . . . Dublin, 1725.

(4) Haywood, Mrs. Eliza, *The Tea-Table or A Conversation between Some Polite Persons of Both Sexes at a Lady's Visiting Day*. 4th ed., London: printed and Dublin reprinted, 1725.

(5) ———, *The Parliamentary Right of the Crown of England Asserted in the Debate at Large Between the Lords and Commons* . . . 3rd ed., London, 1714.

(6) [Vanbrugh, John], *The Country House* . . . Dublin, 1719.

Copies at Columbia University Library;* Cambridge University Library.

1727

The / Christian Hero: / An / Argument / Proving that no / Principles / But Those Of / *Religion* / Are Sufficient to make a / Great Man. / [rule] / ——— *Fragili quærens illidere dentem* / *Offendet solido* ——— Hor. / [rule] / The Eighth Edition. / [rule] / *London*: / Printed for J. Tonson in the *Strand* [short rule] / MDCCXXVII.

Duodecimo.

Signatures: A eight leaves, B–D in twelves, E three leaves.

Pagination: P. [i] Title; p. [ii] blank; pp. [iii–viii], Dedication to Lord Cutts; pp. [ix–xv], Preface; p. [xvi], blank; pp. [1] and 2–78, text. 'Finis' on p. 78. Ornamental initials at the beginning of the Dedication, the Preface, and [Chap. I.]. Head ornaments for the Dedication, the Preface, and each chapter. Tail ornaments following the Preface and 'Finis'.

Copies at University of Texas Library, Aitken Collection;* Library of Congress; Columbia University Library New York Public Library; Cornell University Library; British Museum.

Bibliography

1729

Le / Heros / Chrétien / Par le Chevalier R. Steele. / Traduit de l'Anglois / Par M. A. De Beaumarchais, / Et Les / Vertus Paiennes / Par le Traducteur. / [ornament] / A La Haye, / Chez Henry Scheurleer. / [short rule] / M.DCC.XXIX. /

The title-page is printed in black and red.
Duodecimo.
Signatures: Four unsigned leaves, A–I in twelves, K eight leaves, L twelve leaves, M four leaves.
Pagination: P. [i], Title; p. [ii], blank; pp. [iii–vii], Dedication to Monsieur Le Comte D'Aumale, signed H. Scheurleer; pp. 1–6, Dedication to Lord Cutts; pp. 7–16, Preface; pp. 17–173, text of *Le Héros Chrétien*; pp. 175–231, text of *Les Vertus Païennes*; p. 232, blank; pp. [233–264], Table des Matières.
Library of Congress.*

1737

The / Christian Hero: / An Argument proving that no Principles / But those of / Religion / Are Sufficient / To make a Great Man. / [rule] / By Sir *Richard Steele*. / [rule] / —— Fragili quærens illidere dentem / Offendet solido —— Hor. / [rule] / [ornament] / [rule] / *Dublin*: / Printed by S. Powell, / For George Risk, at *Shakespeeare's head* in / *Dame's-Street*. / [rule] / MDCCXXXVII.

The title-page is printed in black and red.
Octavo.
Signatures: A–D in eights.
Pagination: P. [1], Title; p. [2], blank; pp. [3, 4], Dedication to Lord Cutts; pp. [5–8], Preface; pp. [9] and 10–64, text. 'Finis' on p. 64. Ornamental initials at the beginning of the Preface and [Chap. I.]. Head ornaments for the Preface and each chapter. Tail ornament following the Preface.

Copies at Henry E. Huntington Library;* University of Texas Library, Aitken Collection (title-page missing); Bodleian Library; Cambridge University Library.

1741

The / Christian Hero: / An / Argument / Proving that no / Principles / But Those Of / *Religion* / Are Sufficient to make a /

Great Man. / [rule] / —— *Fragili quærens illidere dentem* / *Offendet solido* —— Hor. / [rule] / The Ninth Edition. / [rule] / *London*: / Printed for J. and R. Tonson in the *Strand*. / [short rule] / MDCCXLI. /

Duodecimo.

Signatures: A eight leaves, B–D in twelves, E four leaves.

Pagination: P. [i], Title; p. [ii], blank; pp. [iii–viii], Dedication to Lord Cutts; pp. [ix–xv], Preface; p. [xvi], blank; pp. [1] and 2–78, text; pp. [79–80], blank. 'Finis' on p. 78. Ornamental initials at the beginning of the Dedication, the Preface, and [Chap. I.]. Head ornaments for the Dedication, the Preface, and each chapter. Tail ornaments following the Preface and 'Finis'. (Ornaments different in design from those of the eighth edition.)

Copies at University of Texas Library, Aitken Collection;* British Museum.

1751 (?)

Allibone, in his *Dictionary of English Literature and British and American Authors*, lists a 1751 edition (8°). George A. Aitken, in his *Life of Richard Steele* (London, 1889), Appendix V, records the 1751 edition as the tenth. Persistent searching, however, has not brought to light a copy of it, and it seems not to have been advertised in the contemporary periodicals. Allibone's statement may be inaccurate in this case as it is in his listing of the 1766 edition as the eighth; and Aitken may have assumed erroneously on the evidence of Allibone's statement that this hypothetical edition was the tenth, following the ninth in 1741.

1755

The / Christian Hero: / An / Argument / Proving that no / Principles / But Those Of *Religion* / Are Sufficient to make a / Great Man. / [rule] / —— *Fragili quærens illidere dentem* / *Offendet solido* —— Hor. / [rule] / By Sir Richard Steele / [rule] / *London*: /

Bibliography

Printed for J. and R. Tonson and S. Draper / in the *Strand*. / [short rule] / MDCCLV. /

Duodecimo.

Signatures: A eight leaves, B–D in twelves, E four leaves.

Pagination: P. [i], Title; p. [ii], blank; pp. [iii–viii], Dedication to Lord Cutts; pp. [ix–xv], Preface; p. [xvi], blank; pp. [1] and 2–78, text; pp. [79–80], blank. 'Finis' on p. 78. Ornamental initials at the beginning of the Dedication, the Preface, and [Chap. I.]. Head ornaments for the Dedication, the Preface, and each chapter. Tail ornaments following the Preface and 'Finis'. (Ornaments slightly different in design from those of the eighth and ninth editions.)

Copies at University of Texas Library, Aitken Collection;* Henry E. Huntington Library; Boston Public Library; University of Wisconsin Library; British Museum.

1756

The / Christian Hero: / An / Argument / Proving that no / Principles / But Those Of / Religion / Are Sufficient to make a / Great Man. / [rule] / —— *Fragili quærens illidere dentem* / *Offendet Solido* —— Hor. / [rule] / The Twelfth Edition. / [double rule] / *Whitehaven*: / Printed and Sold by W. Masheder, 1756. /

Octavo in half-sheets.

Signatures: Four unsigned leaves, B–M in fours, N two leaves.

Pagination: P. [i], Title; p. [ii], blank; pp. [iii–viii], Dedication to Lord Cutts; pp. [ix–xiv], Preface; pp. [1] and 2–85, text; p. [86], blank. 'Finis' on p. 85. Head ornaments for the Dedication and Chap. I.

Bodleian Library.*

1764

The / Christian Hero: / An / Argument / Proving that no / Principles / But those of / *Religion* / Are Sufficient to make / A Great Man. / —— *Fragili quærens illidere dentem* / *Offendet solido* —— Hor. / London, / Printed for T. Wentworth in the Strand. 1764. /

Octavo.

Signatures: [A] eight leaves, B–F in eights. The pages are trimmed so closely that the signature A is lost.

Pagination: P. [i], Title; p. [ii], blank; pp. [iii–viii], Dedication to Lord Cutts; p. [ix], blank; pp. [x–xvi], Preface; p. [xvii], blank; pp. [1] and 2–78, text. 'Finis' on p. 78. No ornaments; no catchwords; very closely trimmed.

The University of Texas Library, Aitken Collection.*

1766

The / Christian Hero: / An / Argument / Proving that No / Principles / But Those Of / *Religion* / Are Sufficient to make a / Great Man. / By Sir Richard Steele. / —— *Fragili quærens illidere dentem* / *Offendet solido* —— Hor. / [double rule] / London: / Printed for J. and R. Tonson in the Strand. / [short rule] / MDCCLXVI. /

Duodecimo.

Signatures: A eight leaves, B–D in twelves, E four leaves.

Pagination: P. [i], Title; p. [ii], blank; pp. [iii–viii], Dedication to Lord Cutts; pp. [ix–xv], Preface; p. [xvi], blank; pp. [1] and 2–78, text; pp. [79–80], blank. 'Finis' on p. 78. Head ornaments for the Dedication, the Preface, and each chapter, different in design from those of the 1728, 1741, and 1755 editions.

Copies at University of Texas Library, Aitken Collection;* University of Chicago Library; Library of Union Theological Seminary, New York.

1766

The / Christian Hero: / An / Argument / Proving that no / Principles / But Those Of / *Religion* / Are Sufficient To Make A / Great Man. / [rule] / —— *Fragili quærens illidere dentem* / *Offendet solido* —— Hor. / [rule] / By Sir Richard Steele. / [rule] / London: / Printed for C. Scott in Fleet-street; and / J. Brown in *Cornhill*. MDCCLXVI. /

Duodecimo in half-sheets.

Signatures: A six leaves, a six leaves, B–M in sixes.

Pagination: P. [i], blank; p. [ii], symbolical frontispiece with the caption: The Christian's Pattern or the Imitation of Christ; p. [iii], Title; p. [iv], blank; pp. [v–xiv], Dedication to Lord Cutts; pp. [xv–xxiv], Preface; pp. [1] and 2–131, text; p. [132], blank.

Bibliography

Finis' on p. 131. Double-rule heading for Dedication, the Preface, and [Chap. I.]. Head Ornament for Chaps. II and III.

University of Texas Library, Aitken Collection.*

1776

The / Christian Hero / An Argument proving that no / Principles / But those of / Religion / Are sufficient / To Make A Great Man. / By Sir Richard Steele. / —— *Fragili quærens illidere dentem* / *Offendet solido* —— Hor. / London: / Printed For T. Pridden, Fleet Street / M. DCC. LXXVI. /

Duodecimo.

Signatures: A–I in twelves.

Pagination: P. [i], Half-title; The Christian Hero; p. [ii], blank; p. [iii], Title; p. [iv], blank; pp. [v, vi], Dedication; pp. [vii–xii], Preface; pp. 13 and 14–108, text. 'The End' on p. 108.

Victoria and Albert Museum, Forster Collection.*

1792

The / Christian Hero: / An / Argument / Proving That No / Principles / But Those Of / Religion / Are Sufficient To Make A / Great Man. / Written by Mr. Steele. / —— *Fragili quærens illidere dentem* / *Offendet solido* —— Ho. / A New Edition. / Berwick: / Printed By W. Phorson Bridge-Street. / MDCCXCII. /

Octavo in half-sheets.

Signatures: A–K in fours, L two leaves.

Pagination: P. [i], Title; p. [ii], blank; pp. [iii–v], Dedication to Lord Cutts; p. [vi], blank; pp. [vii–xi], Preface; p. [xii], blank; pp. [1] and 2–71, text; p. [72], blank. 'Finis' on p. 71. No ornaments.

Copies at University of Texas Library, Aitken Collection;* Library of Union Theological Seminary, New York; British Museum.

1802

The / Christian Hero: / An Argument / Proving That / No Principles But Those of Religion / Are sufficient to make / A Great Man. / [double rule] / By Sir Richard Steele. / [double rule] / —— Fragili quærens illidere dentem, / Offendet solido. Hor. / [rule] /

A New Edition. / [rule] / Oxford: / At The Clarendon Press. / 1802. /

Octavo.

Signatures: a four leaves, b two leaves, c one leaf. B–K in eights, [L] one leaf.

Pagination: P. [i], Title; p. [ii], blank; pp. [iii] and iv–xiii, Preface; pp. [1] and 2–145, text; p. [146], blank. 'Finis' on p. 145. Short double-rule heading for the Preface and Chap. I.

Copies at Massachusetts Historical Society; University of Texas Library, Aitken Collection; British Museum;* Bodleian Library; Cambridge University Library.

1802

The / *Christian Hero*: / Or, No / Principles But Those Of / Religion, / Sufficient To Make A / Great Man. / *Written in the Year* 1701. / [short rule] / By Richard Steele. / [short rule] / "*The world passeth away, and the lust thereof; but he that doeth the will of God abideth forever*". / [double rule] / [ornament] / [double rule] / *Worcester, Massachusetts,* / *From The Press Of* / Isaiah Thomas, Jun. / July —— 1802. /

Duodecimo in half-sheets.

Signatures: A–G in sixes. Only the first and third leaves in each gathering are signed: for example, the first leaf in the second gathering is signed B, the second leaf is unsigned, and the third is signed B 2 [*sic*].

Pagination: P. [i], Title; p. [ii], blank; pp. [iii] and iv–vi, Preface; pp. [7] and 8–84, text; 'Finis' on p. 84. Head ornaments for the Preface and each chapter. Caption for [Chap. I.]: The Christian Hero (instead of the full title). No catchwords. Pp. 81–4 are set in smaller type.

Copies at Harvard College Library;* Boston Public Library; Boston Athenaeum; Princeton Theological Seminary.

1807

The / *Christian Hero*: / an argument, proving that no / principles / but those of / *religion* / are sufficient / to make a great man. / [short double rule] / By Sir Richard Steele. / [short double rule] / —— *Fragili quærens illidere dentem* / *Offendet solido* ——. Hor.

/ [long double rule] / Printed by Smith & Maxwell, / No. 28, North Second Street, / Philadelphia. / 1807. /

Duodecimo in half-sheets.

Signatures: A–I in sixes, K five leaves. Only the first and third leaves in each gathering are signed: for example, the first leaf in the second gathering is signed B, the second is unsigned, and the third is signed B 2 [sic].

Pagination: P. [i], Title; p. [ii], blank; pp. [iii] and iv–vi, Dedication to Lord Cutts; pp. [vii] and viii–xii, Preface; pp. [13] and 14–117, text; p. [118], 'References to Scripture'. 'The End' on p. 117. Caption for [Chap. I.]: The Christian Hero. No catchwords.

Copies at Harvard College Library;* New York Public Library; Library Company of Philadelphia.

1820

The / Christian Hero: / An / Argument / Proving That No / Principles But Those Of Religion / Are Sufficient To Make / A Great Man. / [short rule] / By / Sir Richard Steele. / [short rule] / Embellished with The Author's Portrait. / [short rule] / Bungay: / Published by Charles Brightly. / 1820. / Imprint (p. [ii] and p. 108): J. and R. Childs, Printers, Bungay.

Duodecimo.

Signatures: B twelve leaves, C six, D twelve, E six, F twelve, G six.

Pagination: Frontispiece, verso, Portrait of Steele (Kneller); P. [i], Title; p. [ii], imprint; pp. [iii] and iv–vi, Preface; pp. [7] and 8–108, text; 'Finis' on p. 108, followed by colophon. Caption for [Chap. I.]: The Christian Hero (instead of the full title). Short rule heading for the Preface and for each chapter.

The copy examined is bound in boards with the title printed on the outside as follows:

The / *Christian Hero* / [ornament] / By Sir Richard Steele. / [ornament] / Embellished with the Author's Portrait. / [rule] / Published by C. Brightly, Bungay. /

This is enclosed in an ornamental frame. Outside the frame at the bottom of the page is the imprint: J. and R. Childs, Printers, Bungay.

University of Texas Library, Aitken Collection.*